WHISPERS IN THE BLUE

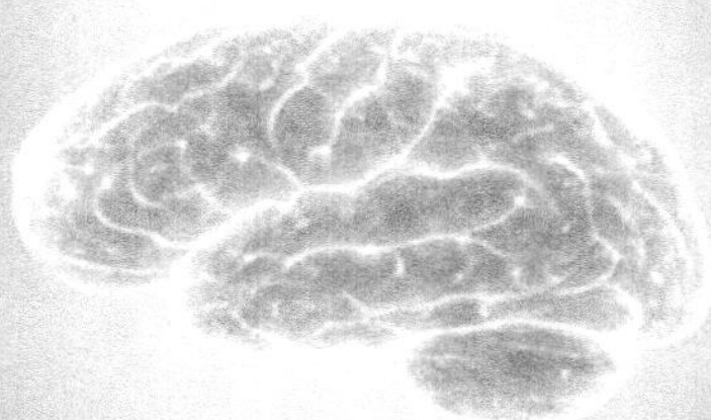

IVY RU

A LIN CITY STORY

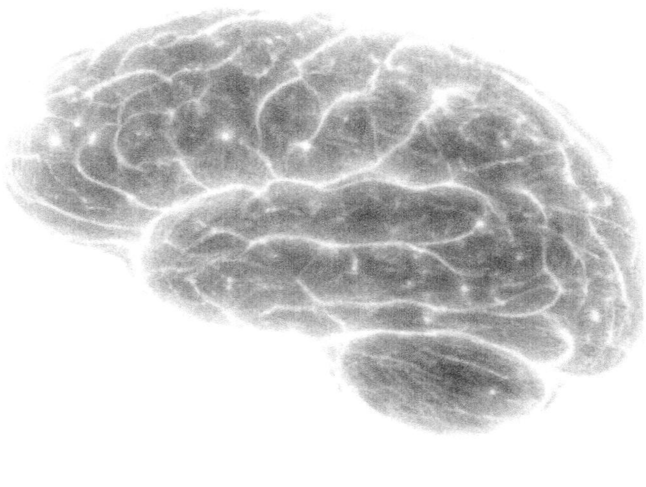

Author: Ivy Ru (IvyRuWrites.com)

Contributing Editor: Jeri Red Shepherd (www.RedWritesBooks.com)

(Digital Blue Background) Futuristic AI Robot with Digital Interface | Gambar Luthfil Aziman Effendi | Canva | Creative Commons

Digital Blue Brain | Sam Seiler | Fiverr

Cover Typography: Sam Seiler, Fiverr

Cover Design: Jeri Red Shepherd

Unpredictable Publishing Logo | Sam Seiler | Fiverr

Lucy's Lantern Literature Logo | Red Writes Books

Nanobot (Cover and Interior): Adobe Stock Image | Creative Commons

Nanotech Logos ("nt" and "Healing Through Innovation" circle) | David Sklenicka | www.DavestarGaming.com | Exclusively License to Ivy Ru Writes and Unpredictable Publishing

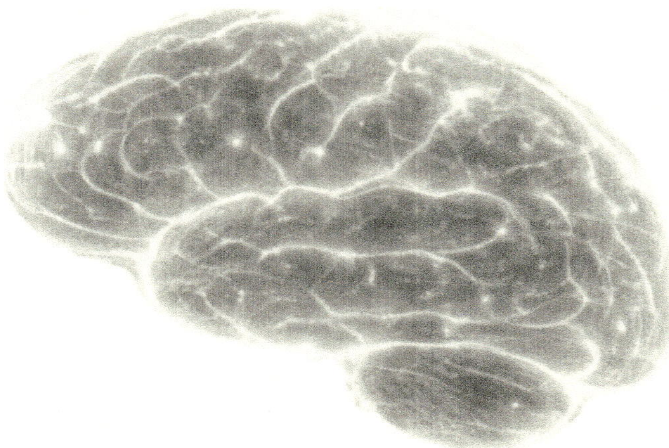

For my Mom and Dad, who always make sure to show they love me no matter what I do in my life.

Thank you for always supporting my weird, often creepy, ideas and my business endeavors.

I couldn't do this without you.

Me with the folks in our Sunday best.

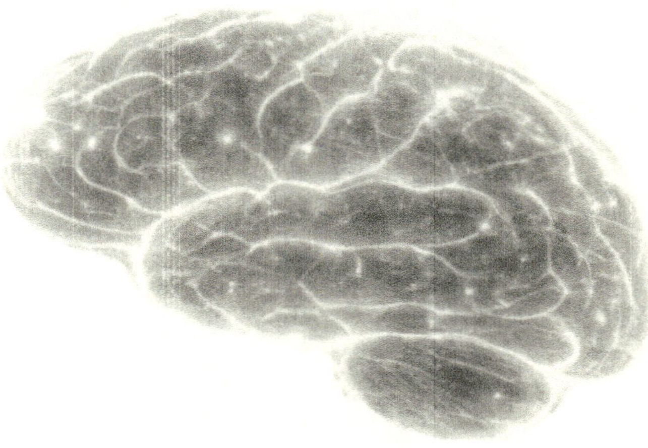

The Unpredictable Author

Whispers In The Blue takes place following the events of *Lin City Stories*, about a month after ***The Call From Below***. You may recognize some characters from other short stories, like Mr. Anderson, but be prepared for a few spoilers if you haven't yet read the prequels.

I want to thank everyone who has read and loved the previous tales of *Lin City*. Your support constantly inspires me, and reminds me to keep my eye on the prize! The prize, of course, is this first finished novel! (For which you should definitely leave me a cool review!)

If you want to stay updated on my future novels, my new *Unpredictable Publishing Label*, and the *Lin City* prequels, or maybe you just want to catch an occasional update from my busy life when I'm not in front of a keyboard, please visit **www.IvyRuWrites.com** to sign up for my newsletter or purchase your own copies of all of the Ivy Ru originals.

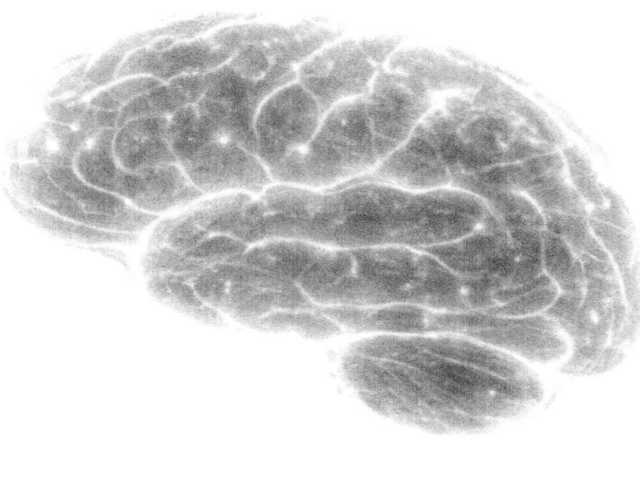

Chapter One

Nanotech Report | Quarter Three

99% of Lin City citizens will have nanobot implants within the next five years

Nanotech Growth in Lin City

In quarter three of this business cycle, we saw an increase of 1.7% in the number of Lin City citizens with nanobots, bringing the total to 95.8%. This includes patients from our newest project that focuses on giving life-saving nanobot treatments to inmates of the Lin City corrections facility. These inmates have faced higher rates of infection in the past, but now can live longer, higher-quality lives. Our economic specialists predict ninety-nine percent of Lin City citizens will have nanobot implants within the next five years.

Innovation

After numerous trials and safety tests, our hardworking biological engineers made it possible for nanobots to locate and eliminate rogue cells in the human body, preventing cancers. We hope to completely stop the creation of mutated cells in high-risk individuals, eventually fully preventing cancerous tumors from forming. We also tested the nanobots' usefulness in cardiac events, and they were successful. We love to hear stories of people who have benefited from their nanobot implants, even though they are not yet as advanced as we will make them someday.

Expansion

As stated in many of our previous reports, the goal of Nanotech is to provide nanobot technology for the entire world and improve the lives of millions. We have begun sending some of our brightest medical professionals and surveyors to take stock of medical facilities and resources in the Rang Provinces. We have already begun communicating with central hospitals in the Rang Provinces, and we hope to start trading nanobots soon.

Thank You

Thank you, Investor, for believing in us and our cause. As always, we are open to feedback and ideas from our investors, and we invite you to join us at our quarterly gala. We will discuss the future of our company and our future relationship with the Rang Provinces and other nations. Your ticket is attached to this message, and we hope to see you there.

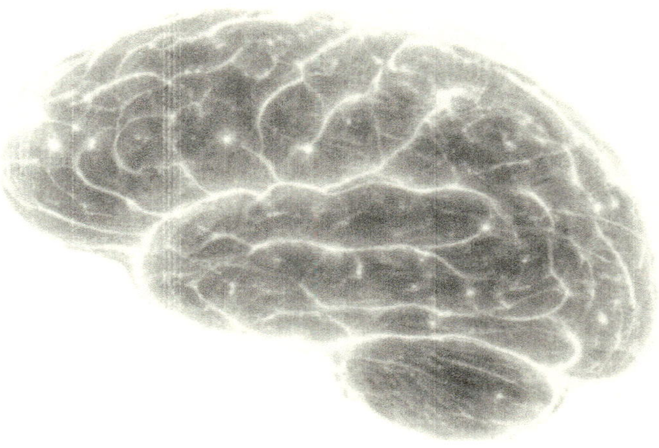

Chapter Two

Uptown

This was the first step into my new life.

My warm and comfortable bed encouraged me to retract my arm as I reached toward my alarm. I randomly pushed a couple of buttons on the blaring device, turning off its incessant buzzing. I rubbed the sleep from my eyes and swung my legs over the side of the bed. My apartment was completely dark, save for the blue streaks of light that had managed to sneak around the edges of my blackout curtains. I stumbled past my closet, not bothering to straighten the bedsheets. My bathroom lights turned on automatically, illuminating the dark circles under my eyes and the unruly cowlicks I had tried so hard to comb flat before I went to bed the previous day.

I inspected myself in the mirror for a moment longer before twisting my hair into a neat bun, using a thick, clear gel I had gotten from one of the Midtown beauty shops to eliminate any unruly strands of hair. I had laid out my suit the night before, when I had stressfully prepared for my day. Even if my alarm had not gone off, I was going to be there on time. I told myself this was normal, that nothing about today should feel scary. It did not work. This would be my first day working in Nanotech, my first day of a new life. I gave a few finishing touches to my look–small gold earrings and shiny new work shoes–before heading back out of my bathroom toward the kitchenette.

I picked up a meal bar from the bowl on my countertop and dropped the shiny blue wrapper into the waste chute on the wall next to me. The meal bar was nothing special: a couple of different kinds of nuts, egg whites, and a preservative with a name I could not pronounce. I ate it quickly, not particularly savoring the bland taste or chewy texture.

I pulled back the curtains over the window by my bed, allowing the artificial light to fill the room completely. All of Midtown and Downtown Lin City had been outfitted with blue streetlights sometime before I could remember. It was meant to increase the productivity of Nanotech employees dealing with the lack of sunlight in the lower levels. It was also meant to keep them awake and alert during long night shifts. According to many of my schoolteachers, the number of work-related injuries had decreased by seventy-five percent after the installation of the blue streetlights. That being said, I was glad to be moving to Uptown for my work. Uptown was the only part of Lin City without the blue streetlights; people could get their energy from the sun like we were supposed to.

The movers had picked up my things a few days ago, so I had nothing left to do in my apartment. Even so, I found it hard to leave. This apartment had been my first solo venture. Not even living in Lin City your whole life could prepare you for living on your own in Uptown. Lin City was so full of life and insanity, but Nanotech brought unity to it.

"Exceptions exist," one of my instructors had said once. "But only until the system notices."

I left my apartment for the last time, hearing the familiar click of the automatic lock.

With my faux-leather briefcase at my side, I ventured out into the city. As the levels of Lin City expanded to what exists today, catwalks and scaffolding were installed, eliminating the need for vehicles or roads. I had heard rumors that the original sidewalks were still intact in Level One, but Level One was just a prison these days, a place that housed some of the most dangerous criminals in the world. No one down there was worried about taking the time to appreciate Lin City foundations.

The sound of my shoes against the metal catwalks joined the cacophony of factory workers returning to their homes after a night shift in one of the Nanotech assembly lines. Nanotech was one of the only industries still running in Lin City; it had offices and factories on every level. The lower levels were home to the more laborious parts of the business, while the intellectual components resided on the upper levels. The Nanotech complex, the center of everything in the company, was on the twelfth and top level. This meant that my commute today would be full of stairs and sharp corners.

I had never been to the top level of the city, and I had not been to Uptown since it became a semi-restricted area, open only to those whose ID cards had been approved by the mayor of Midtown. Most of the time, the only people allowed to enter Uptown were Lin City employees.

I could feel a shift in the air as I moved up through the city and was glad that my new suit jacket provided much-needed warmth. I had forgotten that being up so high was different after being in Midtown. It made me think about how warm it must be in Downtown.

Uptown was blocked by a large gate, making it a quite literal interpretation of a gated community. Everything was separated, clean lines and perfect organization.

Once I reached the entrance to Uptown–Levels Ten, Eleven, and Twelve–I produced my Lin City ID card. One of the guards swiped it through a scanner. A light on the front of the scanner blinked green for a few seconds before the guard returned my card and pushed another button next to the gates.

The gates slid open silently, welcoming me into Uptown and my future.

I stepped into Nanotech and was immediately hit with the scent of the synthetic cleaning product used to clean the catwalks and buildings. The cleaner was heavily lemon-scented, and I finally understood why all of the Nanotech officials had the scent following them. Uptown was also eerily quiet. I looked up as I walked and noticed all of the machinery was wrapped in white and blue striped fabric, muffling any sound that a heater or one of the cleaning robots would have produced.

I felt slightly out of place as I continued up toward Level Twelve, but I tried to shake it off. I probably only felt that way because it was the first day, and my hand-me-down briefcase definitely did not help ward off stares from other citizens. I was distracted from my embarrassment when I first saw the building.

Nanotech Headquarters had always seemed like a faraway castle when I was growing up in Lin City, so seeing it in person was quite surreal. The building was a magnificently tall spire, like a needle poking through the clouds. Almost the entire building was steel or glass, both of which sent blinding reflections of the rising sun in all directions. I took a deep breath and walked toward the front doors, attempting to calm my nerves while also avoiding the rays of light shining toward the ground I walked on.

I held my citizen ID card up to the monitor above the door, and someone inside quickly activated the sliding glass doors. This was the first step into my new life. This was my time.

I stepped inside.

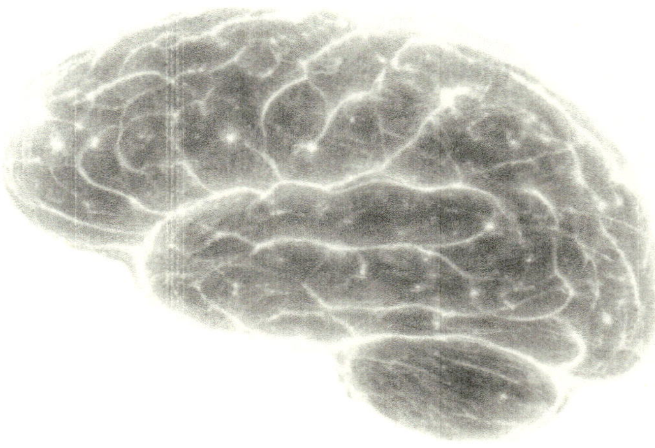

Chapter Three

Beyond The Glass

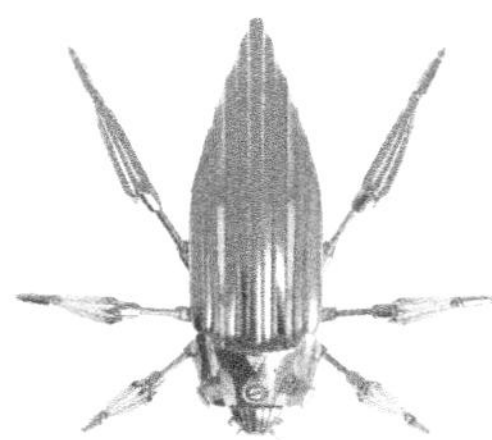

Nanotech tracked everything that mattered.

The interior of Nanotech Headquarters was clean and white, with fresh roses in vases on every available surface. The only other time I had seen roses was at a botanical garden in one of the satellite cities around Nanotech. I went as part of a trip in first school. The botanical garden had since closed, but there must be another flower farmer nearby if Nanotech had such a fresh supply. The roses made me wonder how much of Nanotech's budget went to interior design. I made my way to the front desk and greeted the receptionist with a warm smile, which he returned.

"How can I help you today?" he asked.

"I just arrived for my first day. I'm Mr. Anderson's new assistant," I said, showing him my ID.

He nodded and, after verifying my ID, produced a light blue Nanotech lanyard with my new employee key card and ID hanging from it. I quickly slipped the lanyard around my neck before the receptionist spoke again.

"Welcome to Nanotech, Ms. Carson! My name is Robby. I'm here to answer any questions you might have," he greeted me. "We'll get you set with your security implant here at the end of the day, but your card will work until then," he said before producing a bag, and adding, "I have a few extra things for you. I've put them all in one of our Nanotech tote bags. Mr. Anderson's office is just up those stairs," he said.

I nodded and thanked the receptionist, turning to the grand white stairs. I put my new suit jacket over my shoulder, shifting the weight of my briefcase to the opposite side of my body. The lush carpet on the stairs sank beneath my feet like wet sand. After consulting the map I had been given in my tote bag, I determined the location of My boss's office.

Every door was either white-painted steel or crystal-clear glass. Mr. Anderson's office had a door ornamented by two silver placards, one of which read:

Ellis Anderson, CEO

The other placard stated my name:

Macie Carson, P.A.

I felt a twinge of excitement as I ran my fingers over my name; everything here was so professional, so adult. Just as my hand reached the doorknob, I heard a voice from inside.

"You may enter."

My new office was huge, with windows covering two sides of the room. Mr. Anderson sat at my desk, smiling at me as I entered. We had not yet formally met; a search committee interviewed me for this position, a process for which Mr. Anderson lacked the time.

Mr. Anderson held out his right hand, which I shook. I tried to use the firm-but-friendly grip I had practiced for hours with my parents before my first swimming competition.

“Hello, Ms. Carson. Such a pleasure to finally meet you,” he said, dropping his hand stiffly to his side.

He seemed to assess me. Mr. Anderson did not miss things. He just chose when they mattered. For the moment, I mattered. Did I get the handshake right? I nodded as I tried to form a suitable greeting. The words quickly died in my throat, but Mr. Anderson did not seem to notice.

“The nature of my work at Nanotech means that I need a little extra privacy in my office. You will be in the outer office, welcoming anyone who wants to meet with me and alerting me of their arrival,” he said. "I work in the conjoined office, there," he indicated another door.

“Yes, that is what I understood from my first meeting with the search team,” I confirmed.

“Wonderful. Your selection for this position shows your competence. There is a program on your data screen that should tell you everything you need to know,” Mr. Anderson said, his tone direct but friendly.

I glanced around the room again and waited for him to continue. He did not. Instead, he gestured to the white desk in the middle of the room. I sat and heard his office door close softly behind me.

I scanned my new employee badge in front of the screen, and it promptly unlocked, revealing a larger-than-life nanobot welcoming me.

> ***Hey there, Macie! Whenever you're ready to complete your training as Mr. Anderson's personal assistant, press the confirmation button on your screen.***

I had not expected the training program to be so chipper, but I suppose Nanotech liked to go all out for its employees. I pushed the green symbol on my screen, and it shifted to a view of my home platform. Most of the program was a boring repetition of my year eight computer classes, but I learned a bit about what Nanotech did with its technology.

> ***"Nanotech's systems don't monitor internal behavior," the trainer told us. "Too expensive. Too invasive. Too many false flags."***

Nanotech tracked everything that mattered–movement, access, and health metrics. But not intent. Behavioral monitoring was considered too invasive, too expensive, and too prone to error. At least, that was what the training module said.

I had no idea that Nanotech did so much outreach for understaffed hospitals and less-developed provinces. I also did not know that it was my job to plan welcome parties and organize hotels for heads of those hospitals and leaders of those provinces.

As the program concluded, I received my first assignment: plan a retirement party for Clyde Hansen from IT systems. I also had to organize files and schedule meetings, but those tasks were menial when compared to welcoming a foreign dignitary to Lin City for the first time.

I spent a couple more hours with the system trainer, familiarizing myself with Mr. Anderson's interesting organization choices, before Mr. Anderson emerged from his office.

"Ms. Carson, please feel free to utilize this time to get lunch. There is a cafeteria on Level Nine, but I recommend exploring some of the dining Uptown Lin City has to offer," he said. His voice was rhythmic and monotone, refusing to display a hint of emotion.

I nodded, unsure of what to say in response, and turned off the monitor in front of me. He retreated back into his office. I picked my briefcase up off the floor and left the office uncertainly, trying to decide what to do for lunch. I had not received my chip to unlock my new apartment yet, so I would have to find somewhere else to spend time.

I turned toward the grand staircase after stepping through the office door and was met by a bustling, yet organized group of Nanotech employees. A woman stood at the top of the stairs.

She was dressed in a tailored white skirt suit and cute shoes. The woman smiled when she saw me and waved me over. I started toward her as I racked my brain for any meetings I might be missing.

The woman extended her hand to offer a handshake. I took it.

"Hello, Macie. Remember me? I'm Tasha. I'm a PA for the head of the marketing team now. I recognized your name from second school, and I just wanted to make sure we had a chance to catch up!" she said.

Tasha spoke quickly, so much so that I could barely process what she had said. She laughed like nothing in the world had ever gone wrong. I wondered what it would take to break that. My mind caught up, and I went through my graduating class in my head for a moment, finding Tasha's name.

"Of course. You're Tasha Ali. What brought you to Nanotech?" I asked.

Tasha smiled, clearly thankful that I remembered her so many years later. Tasha began leading me down the stairs as she answered.

"I did an internship program in the marketing sector a couple of years back. My boss decided that I wasn't experienced enough for a job with the senior team, but he offered me a role so I could learn the ropes," Tasha said. She continued to guide me as we exited the building.

I was not used to seeing this much light, and I had to squint my eyes until they were nearly shut just to navigate around the catwalks behind Tasha. She did not seem to notice my discomfort; she continued to tell me all about Nanotech, specifically its marketing sector. The two of us passed rows and rows of apartments, boutiques, and very fancy-looking restaurants before Tasha finally stopped.

We stood in front of a café called The Latte Lounge. The storefront was, of course, mostly white, as was usual in Lin City, but there were strings adorned with many colored flags around the door and windows.

Tasha pulled the door open, causing the little bell above the entrance to jingle on its string. She walked confidently up to the barista, and I followed. I had never thought of myself as a timid person, but everyone in Uptown walked with such confidence, especially Tasha, that it was hard not to straighten my own posture.

"Hello. Today I'm going to need two light lattes and whatever your soup of the day is," Tasha said, like she did not have a care in the world.

We were served our lunch in ceramic mugs and bowls, with untarnished metal spoons. Shops and cafés in Midtown rarely had money to spend on reusable dishware, let alone nice mugs like these. The coffee was sweeter than any I had ever tried, another perk of living in Uptown, I suppose.

As Tasha and I drank our coffees and soup, I wondered why we had never been friends in school. I could almost picture a young Tasha, though I was almost positive we had never met. I was still thankful she had reached out, even if her presence made me question what I truly remembered from my childhood.

I had spent most of my childhood in the one and only swimming pool outside of Uptown. My parents had encouraged me to join the family business of traditional medicine, but they never got me out of the water long enough to teach me anything they wanted to.

I was the best swimmer in Lin City when I was fifteen and the best on the northern continents by the time I was seventeen. I do not swim anymore. I *cannot* swim anymore; at least not competitively. Nanotech was my fresh start, and I was determined to build my life in Uptown.

Chapter Four

An Unexpected Friend

It felt strange to have technology inside me.

I finished my workday in a windowless conference room, taking minutes for a meeting Mr. Anderson was managing. I typed furiously into my datapad during everything; I was not used to being this active with my fingertips. Thankfully, the meeting was not too long, though my fingers still felt like they were going to fall off at any second, and the lack of windows did not help my overall boredom. Who knew that stuffy men in suits tighter than their toupees would be such a drag?

Tasha was waiting for me outside of my office when I returned from the meeting.

"Hey, Macie. I was just looking at some of the new Nanotech mailing info, and it turns out we're neighbors! I can totally walk you to your apartment today. I know Uptown can be a bit confusing for newcomers," she said, her voice just as quick and bubbly as it had been hours earlier at lunch; she didn't seem as worn out as I felt.

"I really appreciate that. Thanks, Tasha. Let me grab my bag from my desk," I replied.

Tasha nodded, and I quickly unlocked the office door with my employee badge. The setting sun was visible from my desk, and I paused, staring at the orange sky. I could not help but fixate on the fiery colors shifting and dancing as the sun sank lower on the horizon. Mr. Anderson's approaching me pulled me from my trance. I began gathering my things from my desk, but Mr. Anderson spoke, his voice soft.

"I remember the first time I ever watched the sunset. I was younger than you are now, and Lin City was only ten levels. I thought the sky was the most beautiful thing I would ever see, and I knew I wanted to touch it someday. Goodnight, Macie."

Mr. Anderson continued past me into his office, only looking back to glance at the sunset again, his eyes full of longing. He had been the head of Nanotech for as long as I could remember, a powerful figurehead. I seemed to have forgotten that he was a person, too.

I slung my bag over my shoulder and walked out of my office, watching the door lock behind me.

Tasha and I walked toward the receptionist desk to get my new ID chip, which would replace my keycard and unlock my apartment. Apparently, the chip was a lot more secure than just having a badge or key card. The same receptionist sat behind the desk. I wondered how long his workday was and how many people he saw. Perhaps boredom was not a product of his profession, but just part of his nature.

"Hi again," I said. "I need my new ID chip. Can you give me one here, or is there someone more . . . medical?"

The receptionist gestured for me to hold out my arm, and rolled the sleeve of my suit up to my elbow. He seemed unfazed by my comment, but I could not help feeling bad for my assumption. His hands were thin and bony, like ice picks against my warm skin.

"I can get that done right now. Just make sure you contact employee support if you have any issues with it."

I nodded. Robby pulled a small silver cylinder from under the desk and pressed the cold metal to the skin right below my elbow.

"This may sting for a moment," Robby said as he steadied my arm against the table between us.

I felt the chip enter my skin, and tears formed in my eyes as it broke through layers of muscle. For a moment, everything around me seemed to dim. The fluorescent lights were not as bright, and the dozens of computers hummed softly. I blinked quickly, forcing away the blue from my vision. The metal cylinder was lifted from my skin. My senses returned to normal. Maybe he should warn people about side effects before implanting the chip.

It felt strange to have a piece of technology in me. I was familiar with Nanotech products, but I had never been allowed a procedure of any kind as a child.

Robby quickly applied an adhesive bandage over the implantation site. Tasha helped me pull down my sleeve as I thanked him. His only response was a nod. I realized that Tasha had been talking to me about the best grocery stores in Uptown as we turned away. I must have tuned her out.

The walk to my apartment was generally uneventful, but Tasha had not lied about Uptown being confusing. Apparently, the original design of Uptown had only planned for a handful of Nanotech housing units, but as the company grew, so did its need for compact but well-appointed apartments. The levels had been expanded quickly, not giving enough time for designers to plan the most efficient placement for the catwalks.

Our housing unit was number eight, one of the oldest on the level. Apparently, this was usual for new employees. If you stayed with Nanotech, you would be moved to newer, more updated apartments throughout your employment. I thought about what Mr. Anderson's apartment might look like; it probably was not even on the same level as the rest of us. I knew if I were him, I would want to be able to watch the sunrise every morning and the sunset every night.

Tasha and I walked silently to our apartments. I was completely drained from the day. I hoped it would get easier, but I could not think of how.

My apartment door slid open when I scanned my new chip, revealing a clean kitchen and living room. The appliances were a little outdated, but all of the furniture had been newly upholstered for my arrival. All of my belongings had already been delivered and organized. My grandmother's lamp sat next to the white couch, looking out of place with its colorful fabric shade. I found a fresh load of groceries in the fridge, with a note from the HR team welcoming me to Uptown.

I did not bother to make a real meal and instead settled for noodles and cheese, which I heated up in the inductive pot I had bought for my first apartment. It was not the most advanced, but I did not feel like figuring out my new fancy stove tonight.

I got ready for bed quickly, thankful that I did not have to unpack anything. I crawled under my covers and noticed that they had given me new sheets. They were a blend of cotton and linen, two things not available outside of Uptown for something as simple as bedsheets.

I fell into darkness as soon as my head hit the batting-filled pillows.

When I woke, I felt like I was in a dream. Even though it was early and most of the city was still asleep, warm sunlight spilled into my apartment. I could barely contain my grin as I got ready for the day.

There were already a handful of my new coworkers milling around the lobby, all dressed in grays and blue. One person, sitting in a chair and reading something off his datapad, caught my eye. He wore a light gray suit like everyone else but had a bright orange scarf wrapped around his head. He looked up and met my gaze with a smile and a wave. I waved back but did not walk over. He was probably busy, and it was not like I did not have somewhere to be.

Mr. Anderson was waiting for me again when I entered. I had not realized I was still smiling until that moment, but I could not bring myself to stop. This life, and these people, felt so far apart from how I thought my life would be . . . and I loved it. I knew then that the previous day's worries were unfounded. The next few weeks flew by and I settled in without reservation.

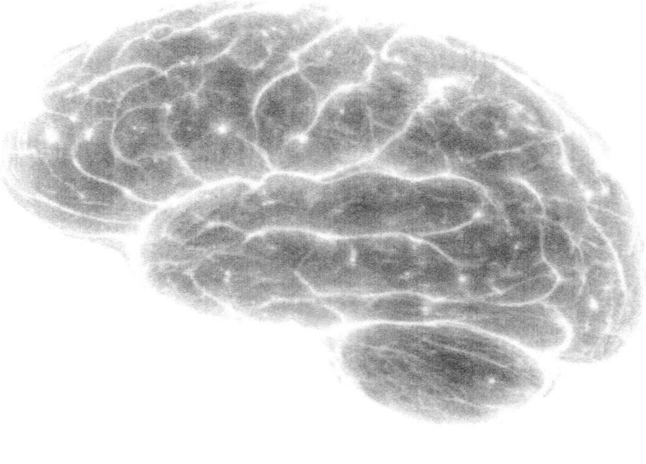

Chapter Five

The Man In The White Helmet

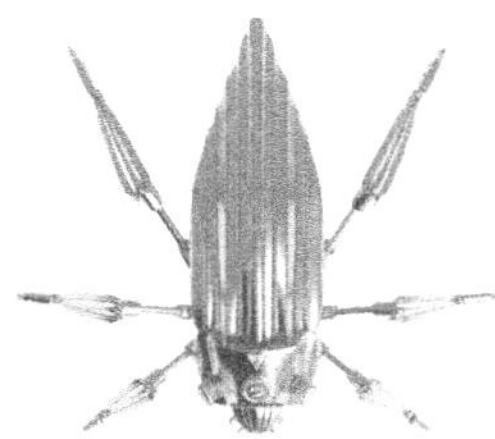

Something about this felt wrong.

Walking through Level Twelve in the morning was a surreal experience. It should have been dark, seeing as the sun had not yet risen and there were no blue streetlights in Uptown, but everything was cast in eerie shadows from the blue lights below. It was as if we hovered above a glowing blue ocean that constantly shifted as shadows and people moved through it. Even though I had been working at Nanotech for almost four months, I still found my walk into work each morning strangely exciting.

My alarm went off early in the morning, and I donned my best pair of walking shoes with my navy suit. Mr. Anderson was stuck in meetings all day and had asked me to do some errands around Uptown. Picking up gifts for foreign dignitaries would be a welcome break from the hours I usually spent in front of my screens.

Nanotech was always quiet when I came in early, but Robby always greeted me with a nod. Tasha had convinced me to join her and Robby "out on the town" more than a couple of times over the past weeks, and I realized that he was not as drab as I first thought, even if he was not quite the life of the party. I stopped at the small café in the lobby and picked up two coffees before heading up to my office–a mocha for me and a black coffee for Mr. Anderson, three creams and two sugars for him.

Before I could find my way upstairs, a woman in the café waved me over. I glanced around, checking that she was not talking to anyone else before walking over, coffees in both hands.

"You must be Macie!" she said. She took a sip of her drink, the buffer giving me enough time to figure out who she was.

I had seen her face many times, in the photo frame on Mr. Anderson's office wall. The picture featured Mr. Anderson and this woman in a greenhouse, probably at the national botanical gardens.

"I am. It's nice to finally meet you, Ms. Hirvonen."

Andrea Hirvonen looked surprised that I recognized her, but pleased.

"Has Mr. Anderson talked about that much?" she asked, trying to hide her obvious pride behind a laugh.

"He talks about your trip to the botanical gardens all the time. He's very fond of you and your family."

This was not true. Mr. Anderson was far too busy saving lives to share anecdotes, but shareholders loved to hear that someone like him talked about them.

"Well, I better let you get back to your office then. Give him my regards!" Andrea said.

I nodded and smiled before resuming my morning routine. This interruption was not unwelcome; it had given me the chance to prove my memory of things Mr. Anderson might not even remember.

I glanced around the lobby again, trying to locate the next part of my routine–the man with the scarves. No, I still had not learned his name, but it had become habit to give him at least a friendly nod before seeing Mr. Anderson. He was nowhere to be seen. I shrugged and assured myself that he must have caught something; the chill of Uptown never helped with colds.

The lights automatically turned on in my office when I stepped inside. I could tell the cleaning crew had been through the night before, and I hoped I remembered to check the lock on Mr. Anderson's adjoining office when I left the previous evening. He hated anyone touching his office, let alone trying to clean it. I was allowed to enter only when he called. That was one of the many peculiarities I had learned about Mr. Anderson.

I set down my things and logged into my data screen. A new message blinked in my inbox, and I opened it. The email was a list of errands for me. The dignitary of the Southern Rang Province was visiting on business, so I was to book a place for her to stay, arrange any transportation she might need, and purchase a welcome gift. I also had to buy decorations for my second employee-departure party. Doug Hastings' was retiring from the marketing department. Not the most exciting day, but I had been wanting to get a better look at Uptown rather than just the restaurants Robby and Tasha frequented.

I left the office around eight o'clock, just as Mr. Anderson was coming in. He trusted me now, and we exchanged friendlier greetings.

"Good morning, Macie," he said.

"Good morning, Mr. Anderson. I have your coffee right here," I responded, holding out the cub for him to take into his office.

Mr. Anderson nodded. "I trust you've checked the message I forwarded to you?"

"Of course," I said.

"I will return this afternoon. I'll leave the gifts with the front desk," I added.

Once Mr. Anderson gave a nod of approval, I walked past him but stopped short. I noticed a large, dark splotch on his tie; it was an uncharacteristic lapse in cleanliness. He seemed very disturbed when I pointed it out. I didn't intend to embarrass him, so I hurried away to let him recompose himself.

I knew that getting lost in Uptown would not be an issue for me. I had always been good at memorizing maps and mazes, even as a young child. It had taken me a couple of weeks to memorize the maps for Uptown, but—once I did—I could walk confidently through the catwalks.

My first stop was a small boutique near the transport platform. It was not somewhere many locals shopped, but it had proven to be a treasure trove for welcome gifts. There were small metal models of Nanotech Headquarters, blue T-shirts with Lin City printed on them in different fonts, and dishware etched with the Lin City crest or the Nanotech logo. I chose a few trinkets from the shop, wrapping everything in thin paper and placing it into a larger metal basket painted blue and labeled with the dignitary's name, her dates of arrival and departure, and the Nanotech logo. Sometimes I forgot which symbol was the Lin City crest and which was the Nanotech logo. The city and the company seemed to go hand in hand after functioning together for so long.

The basket bounced against the outside of my leg as I continued through Uptown. I was sure that I would find a bruise when I went to bed later. My next stop was the temporary apartments. There were three buildings that were permanently reserved for high-profile Lin City visitors. I had never been inside before that day, but I had heard that they were much nicer than any of the employee housing units. I only saw the lobby, but I could tell that the rumors were true.

Instead of the slate gray and blue of the employee housing, everything in the luxury building was white and seemed to shimmer in the sunlight.

Making a reservation was easy, and I arranged for the gift basket to be left in the dignitary's room by the housekeeping staff. I also reserved a couple of rooms for the dignitary's security. It was custom in the Southern Rang Provinces for any political figures to travel with a team of at least four Rang officers. This was something I had learned after the last time a Rang official had stayed in Lin City. We had to message the temporary housing, begging for two additional rooms. I cringed as I left the reservation office, remembering the embarrassment of that visit.

A shift of guards was headed to lunch, all dressed in fitted white uniforms and helmets. A few were jostling each other around and laughing, threatening to push each other off the catwalks. I smiled and nodded as I passed them. Many of the guards stepped aside as I passed; my high-level Nanotech ID badge encouraged that reaction from people outside of the office.

I began walking toward my last stop, Lin City Bakery, to schedule the cake for Doug's party when I noticed one guard had split from the rest and was following me. I looked back at him for a moment but shook off the initial fear of being followed. The guards were only here to survey the city and prevent crime, especially in Uptown.

I took a sharp turn toward the bakery and noticed that the guard was edging closer, taking long strides to catch up to me. The young man, upon noticing my glance toward him, waved in a friendly manner with a gloved hand.

I stopped, waiting for him to reach me. Something about all of this felt wrong, but I could not explain why, and that made it worse. The way he was looking at me was not casual. It was focused, as if he had already decided something.

"Macie Carson," the guard said under his breath as he approached. Then, louder, "We've had higher levels of theft in Midtown recently. We are increasing security throughout the city. Part of this means that we want everyone to travel in pairs. If you don't have anyone to walk with, I would be happy to accompany you."

The man removed his helmet. He had buzzed hair like the rest of the Lin City Guard, and he had a face that commanded a certain level of respect. I had definitely been hit on by worse.

"I didn't know crime had become so common. I'm just heading to Lin City Bakery. I appreciate the offer, but I'll be fine," I said, turning from the guard and walking away.

I heard the guard sigh behind me, but he did not follow. At least he knew how to handle rejection.

"Stay safe out there, Macie," he said, a defeated tone in his voice.

My badge was still clipped to my jacket. Of course he knew my name. That did not make it feel any better. But as I blinked, I noticed that the badge was turned around, unreadable. It took me a moment to recognize his mistake, but once I did, I froze and turned back to look at him. This kind of slip-up was what you were supposed to notice according to all of those late-night crime reports. The guard looked completely unbothered as he slid his helmet under his arm. I thought back to my months in Uptown. Did I really know this guy? My heart caught in my throat, and my voice cracked as I spoke again.

"How do you know my name?" I asked, my heart beating rapidly.

The guard froze for half a second, like he had not meant to say it, much less twice. His eyes flicked past me, checking something. Then his expression hardened, and he sprang into action. The guard barreled toward me, discarding his helmet on the catwalk. I turned and fled, weaving through Level Twelve, hoping that my knowledge of every dead end would help me get away from the clearly deranged guard.

Visions of dead bodies found in dumpsters flashed through my mind, urging me to run faster. I made the mistake of looking back, checking to see if the guard was still behind me. This moment of distraction made me miss a set of stairs, and I tumbled, falling flat against the perforated metal landing. My head spun as I tried to stand, but the guard was on top of me in a second. I flailed wildly, trying to free myself.

"Macie, listen to me," the guard said, his breath tight. "I don't have time to explain this. Others are already watching you."

His words barely registered as I continued to writhe. His padded elbow pressed against the back of my neck, and he swore as something fell to the ground next to my head. A syringe full of cloudy liquid rolled away from us, its needle glinting in the evening light. I attempted a lunge toward the syringe, reaching my free arm toward it, trying to push it over the edge of the catwalk. I could not move at all under the weight of the man, and he retrieved the syringe quickly.

The taste of blood filled my mouth and pooled around the left side of my face. It smelled like iron and rubber. A needle pressed through the skin on the back of my neck as I struggled to turn my head. The guard held me down firmly, and I felt the contents of the syringe mix with my own blood.

Once the guard removed the needle, his grip loosened. My legs slowly stopped kicking. Whatever was in the syringe began to take effect. I felt weightless as I was slung over the man's shoulder. I tried to scream as he wiped my blood from the ground, but no sound came out.

Through a cloud, I glimpsed him tucking away the syringe and gathering his helmet, all with me on his shoulder like a ragdoll.

Soon, all I saw was darkness.

Chapter Six

Rebel, Rebel

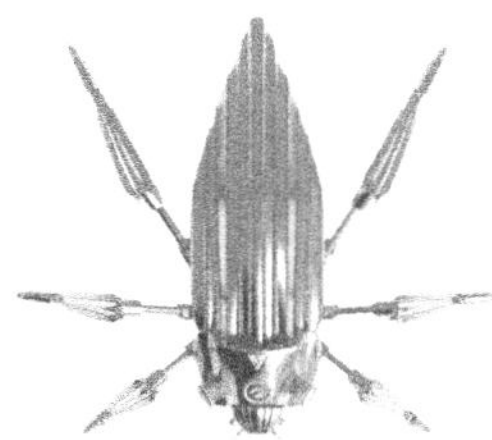

I am not trying to hurt you.

I woke up with a start in a room shrouded in darkness. My hands would not stop shaking–not because of the restraints, but from the realization that nothing I believed about my life was stable anymore. The fake guard must have put me here.

I scanned my body for broken bones and found that my hands and ankles were cuffed to the metal chair I was sitting on. One of my arms was wrapped in a thick cloth band. I also discovered my ankle was throbbing, though I was unable to inspect it in the dark. With a yank, I confirmed that the cuffs were secure. I took a deep breath before continuing my inspection of the surroundings. There was a crack of light in the corner of the room, probably from under a door. Other than that door, all I could sense was the chair I sat in, and shadows vaguely hinted that there was a table in front of me. I did not like not understanding what was happening.

The chair scraped against the floor when I tried to scoot my way toward freedom. Then the door swung open. I was blinded by warm lights, and I squinted, only making out the silhouettes of two people as they entered.

One of the figures turned on a light that I had not noticed before and sat on the other side of the table. As my eyes adjusted, I could see that they were dressed in Nanotech factory uniforms and medical masks that covered the lower parts of their faces. The person across from me stared coolly, with stony gray eyes. I waited for them to speak.

"Hello, Macie. Do you know who we are?"

I shook my head. "Some freaks who want ransom?" I guessed.

The standing figure chuckled, only to be silenced by a look from the person in front of me.

"Not quite," they stated, sliding a datapad across the table for me to read.

"We are members of a top-secret organization. Our aim is only to help the people of Lin City. We think you can help us."

As they finished speaking, I skimmed through the datapad. The display showed a news article from a city in the Rang Provinces. It detailed an apparent blockade of any outside information to Lin City. As I read it, I realized I had really only ever seen Lin City broadcasts that summarized news from the rest of the world. Sure, it was strange, but it was a very efficient way to pass on information, in my eyes.

“The people of Lin City might be better off if you stopped kidnapping them,” I said, tugging again at the cuffs holding back my wrists.

The seated person flicked their hand toward me, and the other walked over. My cuffs were off in an instant, freeing both my wrists and ankles.

“You’re not free,” the standing figure said. “Not yet.”

I flexed my wrists anyway.

“Then why take them off?”

“Because if you’re going to help us,” they replied, “you need to choose it, not survive it.”

I felt a twinge of pain as the ankle cuffs were released, but I tried to hide my gritted teeth behind a scowl. The figures conversed for a moment before taking the datapad back and stowing it in a black bag. The bag was made of the same material as the band around my arm.

“What is this?” I asked, gesturing to the armband.

“That is something our engineers developed. It blocks signals from your implant so Nanotech can’t track it. This is all top secret.”

I nodded. “What does Nanotech have to do with this?”

“You will understand in time, Macie. For now, we will have someone look at your ankle.”

They exited, but left the light on this time.

I mulled over the cryptic conversation while I waited. How had I never heard of anything like this before? No matter how secret something in Lin City was supposed to be, no one here could keep their mouth shut for long.

The shadows of people moving outside the door interrupted the light too often to consider escape. It was not long before another person entered, wearing the same type of mask as the two before. This person spoke in a calmer, less interrogative voice.

"Hello, Macie. I know this is probably terrifying for you, but maybe checking out that ankle can make you a bit more comfortable," they said.

They turned my chair toward them so that my swollen ankle was fully illuminated by the overhead light. My shoes had already been removed, so the person had easy access to my injury.

After only seconds of painful poking and prodding, I got a diagnosis.

"Only a sprain. I'm surprised your nanobots haven't already started healing the area, but I'm sure they will act soon," they said, standing and moving back toward the door.

I stopped them quickly, grabbing the edge of their shirt. "I've never had nanobot injections."

The figure's eyes widened as they turned back.

"I'll see what I can do to get you somewhere more comfortable. This will take time. You may have to stay with us."

I shook my head. "I am not about to form some sort of Stockholm syndrome with you. I'm sure you'll be able to get whatever you want from me quickly and just let me go."

The figure did not respond, and I was left alone again.

Almost everyone in Lin City had nanobot implants by now, and I was supposed to, too. After my shoulder injury in high school, I was supposed to get the injection, but my parents refused to sign. My HR documents were forged so I could get a job

Uptown.job in Uptown. I'd wanted to get a nanobot injection for years, but if anyone found out the earlier procedure was faked, I would never have been able to work for Nanotech.

I did my best not to get injured and to stay away from doctors when I was sick. My plans did not include getting kidnapped, spraining an ankle, and being treated by a random person. In a random room. On a random Level.

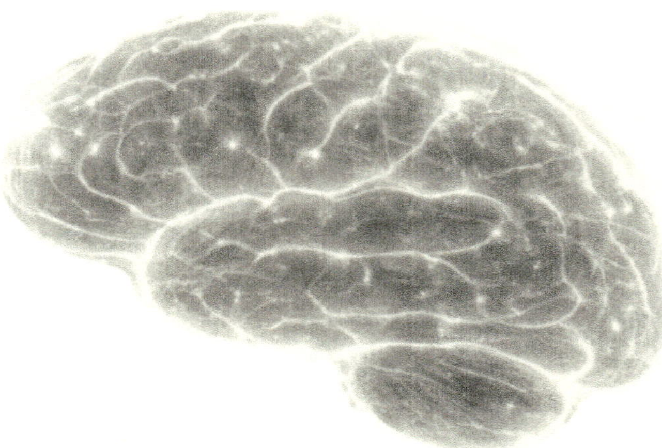

Chapter Seven

Behind The Curtain

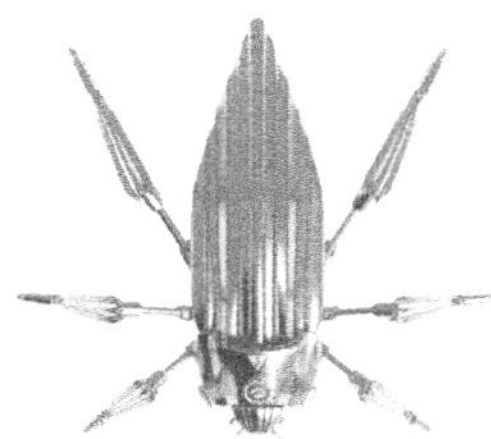

You're already too deep to walk away.

What felt like hours passed before the door opened again. This time, the man who walked in was pushing a rusted wheelchair. Once he had locked the wheels, he offered me a hand, which I thought about refusing, but after testing my ankle, his help seemed like a much better plan. I was not handcuffed to the wheelchair, but there was not much chance of running. If I cooperated now, maybe I could get a good layout of the building. It was my only chance of eventual escape. That being said, something told me this man would not hurt me. Call it intuition.

The wheels squeaked as I was pushed out of the room. It was the only sound other than our breathing. Finally, the man pushing me spoke.

"Sorry about the wheelchair. It's the only one we had down here. We didn't want to make you walk on your sore ankle."

The bright fluorescent lights made me squint as I took in my new surroundings. The walls outside my room were covered in layers of peeling beige paint and tape that poorly concealed cracks. After a few more twists and turns, we stopped in front of a pair of doors. They were made of frosted glass, different from every other door we had seen, and I could hear voices beyond them. One of the doors was pulled open before my companion had the chance to knock. The woman who opened the door lacked the mask that the others had worn.

The woman was older, probably around sixty-five or seventy years old, and she had almost completely silver hair and wrinkles framing her eyes. We were ushered into the room quickly. Whoever had been talking before I entered was silent now. No one was wearing a mask, and I recognized one of them as the faux guard who had attacked me earlier. I sneered at him, and he turned away.

The older woman who had met me at the door spoke first.

"I am sorry for all of this secrecy, Macie. I truly am, but you understand."

I shook my head vigorously. "I really don't, actually. Why exactly did you need to assault and abduct me?" I asked, adding as much bite to my voice as I could muster.

The woman looked disapprovingly at the fake guard before speaking again.

"My name is Dr. Bethel," she said, though it felt like a lie. "This young man next to me is Simon. His plan was to bring you in without a struggle, and your injuries are regrettable."

I stared at Dr. Bethel in disbelief. How could she say something like that? People did not just get abducted, not in Lin City, not in Uptown.

She continued without addressing my expression.

"We had to bring you here to show you the truth about the company and the man who employs you. Do you know what became of your predecessor?"

I shook my head. All I had been told was that the role was open and that I was qualified, and why would I ask more questions about this once-in-a-lifetime offer? This job was my dream; I did not want to ruin it before it even started. When I was younger, my parents hated Nanotech. They were invested in traditional medicine. I paid for their ignorance later . . . *and continued to pay,* I thought, as I flexed my ankle. I knew Nanotech was good, and I knew I could be part of that good. Simon set a steaming cup on the table in front of me. I had not even noticed that he had moved.

"We were able to show your predecessor what was going on in the underbelly of Nanotech. Her name was Aria, but she was caught. They used her nanobot implants to simulate a heart attack. Aria died before she could share anything with the people who most need to know what's going on—the citizens of Lin City."

I turned to look at the person who had pushed me in. His face revealed nothing about the validity of what Dr. Bethel was saying.

"You not being injected with nanobots makes you an even greater asset to our team," Simon said, finally breaking his timid silence. "They can't kill you, or at least they can't make it look like natural causes."

Dr. Bethel nodded in agreement. She moved to the door behind me and opened it slowly. "Adrien, come in," she beckoned.

Another man entered the already cramped room carrying a black metal rectangle the size of his palm. This man looked similar enough to Simon that they could be related, but different enough to tell that they were not the same age. This man was younger, more disorganized. The bag on his back was overflowing with datapads and amateur robotic gadgets.

"I have here a short collection of images and videos concerning the crimes of the Nanotech organization," he said, setting the rectangle onto a side table in the middle of the room.

A circle in the middle of the rectangle lit up, projecting a black-and-white image into the air. There was a portrait-style image of an elderly man, with a ring of hair and sagging cheeks. He had a generically familiar appearance, like an uncle met as a child who still takes up memory space.

"This," Adrien started, "is a picture of Ellis Anderson, your employer, forty years ago."

I scoffed. Mr. Anderson was not quite a young man, but he was not older than his mid-fifties.

"I have to say, your editing skills are great," I said.

Adrien, clearly unphased by my doubt, continued.

"Nanobots were first pioneered by Ellis Anderson and Doctor Mari Nev as an age-reversal product that used telomere protection technology. It extends lifespans by preventing and reversing cellular degradation. That's how Ellis Anderson returned to the appearance we recognize today, but he still needed more.

"Now, nanobots have become a miracle solution to any ailment. Every Nanotech employee is required to have them, except, for some reason, you."

I did not have anything to say now. These people did not need to know anything about me, and they especially did not need to know anything about my lack of nanobot implants. I regretted letting that slip earlier

"Using employees of Nanotech and the prisoners on Level One, Anderson and Dr. Nev were able to start experiments on human patients. The goal was to improve the bots' healing capabilities and to stabilize age retention. Those experiments continue."

The image that appeared next was a man lying on a table wrapped in white paper, tubes and wires covering every inch of exposed skin. His face was contorted into a scream, his eyes wide and frightened. A shiver trickled down my spine as I made eye contact with the image.

While the image flickered in front of me, I could barely register anything that was being said. Could Mr. Anderson really do something like this? Even if the first picture was doctored, the man looked so real, his expression of pain so genuine.

Before I could fully process what I was seeing, another image flashed into the air.

"This is a post-mortem photograph of Aria Stao, the woman who was killed while working as Mr. Anderson's personal assistant–the job you now hold. She was contacted by the rebellion and given the same information about the experiments that you now posess. When her nanobot implants were used to trigger a heart attack. She died in her office."

This image was of a young woman, her face calmer than the man before. I had not heard anything about Mr. Anderson's previous assistants. I assumed they had just transferred to a different city, which was why I never ran into them around the office. Maybe they found a better opportunity in the outreach sector of Nanotech. How could her death have been hidden so well?

I realized, after a moment lost in my own thoughts, that Adrien was still talking. He said something about the body, but I could barely hear him. I do not know how much time passed before he showed me the next image. Nausea rose to my throat when I saw the newest figure. A familiar, but bloodied man lay on a plastic-wrapped bed, his throat adorned with a colorful silk scarf.

Chapter Eight

The Choice

I couldn't tell where the fear started.

I sat in stunned silence after Adrien concluded his presentation. The final images showcasing the aftermath of a nanobot attack still flickered in the air in front of me. Even when I closed my eyes, the scarved man's contorted face was burned into my vision. I had not even learned his name.

Dr. Bethel waved at Adrien, and he turned off the projection. Was it possible that the images I had seen could have been fabricated? The thought floated through my mind, but I could not make it true. Those people were real. They had names, lives, and a scarf collection. I blinked away my tears before they could fall.

Adrien placed the projector in his backpack, fished out a datapad, and handed it to me.

"I put together all of the pictures and news articles and stuff that I just showed you, in case you wanted to take a look for yourself," he said. "It's a lot to take in. The first time I saw some of this stuff, it took me days to accept any of it."

"Thanks," I said, unsure of what to do with this information. I had barely processed anything in the past fifteen minutes.

The entire room sat in silence, as if waiting for me to speak. I did not. Eventually, Dr. Bethel broke the silence with a clap of her leathery hands. The other members left, leaving just the doctor and me.

"You knew the last victim, correct?" she asked.

I shook my head, looking down at my hands. "No. Not really."

Bethel reached out, holding my clasped hands in hers. "Nanotech has affected the lives of everyone here, and everyone you will meet. You might not have known his name or his job title, but you saw him. You saw him in a way that Nanotech never could."

I did not respond. This woman did not know me, so why was she saying these things?

"We do have a few things for you to consider, but for now, let's have a meal. It is always best to break bread with those we want to call friends."

Dr. Bethel stood slowly, using the arms of her chair to assist her ascent. She walked behind my chair and wheeled me out of the room.

"Emmalyn," Dr. Bethel nodded to a muscular woman dressed in black waiting beside my door.

Of course they still had security on me. It was silly to think that it was really just Dr. Bethel and me. Emmalyn took over the task of pushing me through the hallways between aged walls with peeling paint. Her footsteps echoed and the rhythmic squeaking of the old wheelchair made my brow ache. Or maybe my brow was aching from the stress of wondering if I was on the menu for the meal or not. I do not know how many people worry about cannibalism day to day, but it is probably not enough.

We reached a yellowed fiberglass door with a plastic placard next to it that read: Dining Hall. I could hear laughter, and warmth bled through the door as my hand brushed against it. I was pushed inside, and the cacophony ceased. Instead of joy, I was met with stares and whispers. Emmalyn positioned me at one end of a long table. Both sides were outfitted with retractable bench seats, so the end was the only place I fit while in the wheelchair.

The food around the room looked edible enough, but the cans it appeared to come from did not look completely sanitary. A faint metallic smell clung to the air, something just sharp enough to make me question the hunger I just realized I was experiencing. I glanced around the table, surveying the faces of the other "recruits." Most of them wore welcoming smiles, though they had grown quiet. The sounds of scraping spoons and metal on metal resumed, as Dr. Bethel took the seat next to me. Her meal had already been waiting for her.

"Matthew, join us," she said to a man at the stovetops. He came over with two more bowls of the mystery food, as well as spoons.

Reluctantly, after Matthew and the doctor began eating, I scooped up a chunk of meat, and briefly inspected it before deciding it was better than starvation. I may have been wrong. I choked down the lukewarm stew, and the texture sat heavy on my tongue. I had to force myself not to gag. Around me, spoons scraped against bowls in uneven rhythms, too loud, too constant, and filling the room in a way that made it hard to think.

Dr. Bethel recognized the tension and stood to formally introduce me. "Good evening, everyone. This is Macie Carson. We are trying to make her feel as at home as possible," she said.

As if it was an order, the hum of the dining hall returned and Matthew, across from me, spoke softly. He wasn't really whispering, but I had to lean closer to hear him over the conversations that returned to the room.

"Have you ever been to lower levels, Macie?"

I shook my head. I had never traveled lower than the seventh level, let alone into Downtown.

"Well, I hope this food is up to your expectations. If you need anything, just let me, or any of us, know, and we'll do our best," Mathew said with a smile.

He turned to the woman sitting next to him, and smiled, as if telling her it was her turn to talk to the new girl.

"Hi, Macie! I'm Beatrice. We met earlier. We talked a bit about your ankle. You're from Uptown, right?"

I nodded. "Yeah, I'm in one of the Nanotech employee housing units right now."

I did not know why I chose to be honest. I could have lied. Beatrice looked at me, though, in a way that made me think she really cared. I knew that part of me would have felt guilty if I had hidden the truth.

"Oh, a nice gray box, then!" Beatrice joked. She spoke like we were friends. I could not help but let out a small laugh.

"Sure, but it's my gray box."

Dr. Bethel chuckled softly, smiling at Beatrice as she returned to her seat.

The people around me settled into small talk, which I occasionally chimed in on. It felt strange to eat with a group. I had become so accustomed to eating alone in Uptown. Aside from the hurried lunch breaks I took with Robby and Tasha—never longer than half an hour—none of us ever shared a meal together.

Emmalyn sat nearby, and even she cracked a smile from time to time. These people were happy to just sit around a table for hours, long after they had finished their food. Eventually, a few people rose from the table to collect bowls, while others wiped the table clean with rags and recycled water.

Before standing, Emmalyn leaned toward Dr. Bethel, and whispered something into her ear.

Dr. Bethel nodded and sighed. She turned toward me.

"Macie, I wanted to wait to bring this up with you. You've already dealt with so much today, but Emmalyn thinks it's important to decide."

My heart jumped behind my ribs. "Decide what?" I asked, my voice wavering slightly. After the meal, I had almost forgotten how I had gotten here and what these people could do to me.

"We need you to decide whether or not you'll help us. If you do, we'll help you get back into Uptown to collect intel on your boss, Mr. Anderson. If not, we'll have to take some more creative measures."

"You won't be alone," Emmalyn added. "You'll be monitored the entire time."

“What are these creative measures?” I asked.

Adrien spoke up, swallowing a quick gulp of tea before opening his mouth.

“Well, we have technologies that can alter, or erase, part of your memory. But we don’t want to use those. It would make us no better than Nanotech. Especially if it was unsuccessful We want you to work with us. We know that you can help us make a difference.”

I felt a chill at the base of my skull. At least they wouldn't outright kill me, but I imagined what an "unsuccessful" use of the technology Adrien described might be. Maybe, if this technology was real, I could go back to my life. I did not want to forget what I had seen, though. I did not want to forget that bloodstained scarf.

“You’re asking me to betray the only system that works in this city,” I said.

“But who is it working *for*?” Dr. Bethel replied.

The room fell silent.

I pictured Uptown—clean air, sunlight, order.

Then I pictured the man on the table, the one who could not stop screaming.

My hands tightened in my lap. My breath caught, shallow and uneven, as if my body already understood the cost before I did.

“If I go back,” I said slowly, “and you’re wrong. I lose everything.”

Dr. Bethel did not answer.

“But if you’re right,” I continued, “everyone else already has.”

I closed my eyes for a moment, the image of the bloodstained scarf flashing behind my lids.

"I'll do it," I said. "I'll help you."

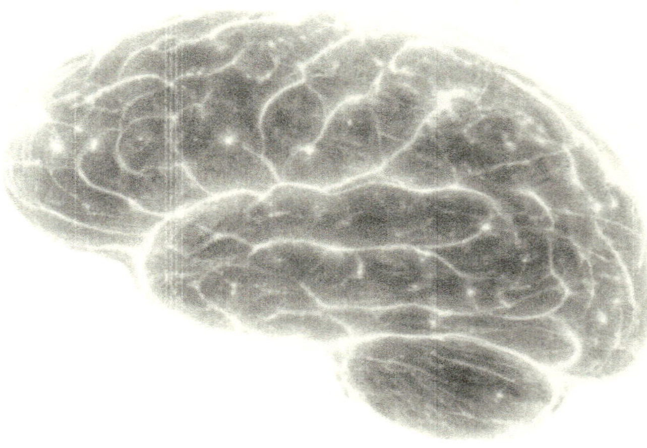

Chapter Nine

Downtown

Every step I took had already been logged.

Adrien pushed me from the dining hall after everyone had finished clearing the tables. Everything that followed happened in less than a week. There had been some arguing over how much security was needed, but they finally came to the conclusion that I could not get anywhere quickly while I was injured. Not like I could find my way out anyhow. Everything here was a labyrinth of low ceilings and sharp corners. I had begun to piece a few different landmarks together, but without any way to record them, I would have to guess the rest.

Adrien spoke as we walked, trying to encourage some form of small talk.

"Not every member of the rebellion is required to live at HQ. We actually encourage people to keep their homes when they join. If you do decide to join the rebellion, you will have a unique situation, being that you live the farthest away from headquarters."

I nodded, but I did not hear much of what he was saying. I could not stop thinking about everything I had heard and seen that day. How could I turn my back on the company that saved the lives of so many and gave such amazing opportunities to the people of Lin City? After seeing the experiments, though, how could I not?

Adrien unlocked a fiberglass door, identical to the others lining the halls. I looked past him as the door opened, surveying the room before we entered. Now that I knew I was in Downtown, the lack of natural light made more sense. Adrien maneuvered the wheelchair into the room, wedging it between the wall and the bed. The room was small enough that the two of us felt like a crowd. He moved to leave, but I grabbed his arm, forcing him to make eye contact with me.

"You have to tell me now if this is real. If you have any inkling that anything I've seen today has been a lie, I need to know."

Adrien waited for a moment before responding, his face serious. His eyes were warmer than the others I had met. He did not hate or fear me. Not yet.

"It's all true, Macie, even though I wish it wasn't. No one here will lie to you, I promise," he said.

I let go of his arm, letting my hands fall back into my lap. He held my gaze for a moment longer before leaving the room. The door clicked softly behind Adrien, but he did not lock it. These people seemed so paranoid, yet so trusting. I wondered how many lived in the complex, like Adrien had suggested. There could not have been more than half a dozen rooms in the hallway mine was in. Perhaps this was all there was in the "rebellion." I could not imagine dedicating my life to fighting an unwinnable battle.

I did not sleep much that night. I tossed and turned in the rough sheets constantly, and tried to pull off the arm cuff every hour or so, but no matter how many angles I tried, it still refused to budge. Eventually, I gave up on the cuff and opened the tote bin next to my bed. I assumed it would be empty, but the bottom was covered in a layer of one-size-fits-all clothes and general survival gear. I pulled out a flashlight, a metal thermos, and a set of two isobutane canisters still in their protective plastic. All of the extra clothing was a shade of gray that reminded me of ash, the kind that blew through Midtown after forest fires.

I picked up the flashlight, and it flickered on in my hand. The light was dim, but helpful in the darkness. My ankle still throbbed slightly, but I was able to push myself onto my feet and toward the door. Every step I took caused another creak in the floor, but everything seemed louder at night. Pushing open the door as quietly as possible, I stepped into the hallway. The building I was in seemed to be a retired business of some kind, with public restrooms at the end of each hall and large meeting rooms now used for storage. The only windows were in the front lobby, where the glow from the blue streetlights was blocked by thick pieces of cloth and tape covering the glass. I walked toward one of the covered windows, turning off my flashlight.

Lifting up the corner of the cloth cover, I caught a glimpse of Downtown. There was barely any movement, but I could see a few lights flicking on and off in the apartments across the catwalks. I wondered if the people living in those apartments knew what was happening in the offices right across from their front doors.

“Can't sleep?” I heard.

I flinched at the voice behind me, startled by the break in the silence. An older man joined me at the window. He smiled gently and said, "I'm Stephen."

“I never sleep well in new places, especially not after everything you showed me,” I said, dropping the makeshift curtain back to the wall.

Stephen was silent for a moment. I could barely make out his face in the darkness.

“Whenever I can’t fall asleep, I go to the dining hall and make a nice cup of tea. I can show you where we keep the mugs if you’re interested,” he said, beckoning me toward the rebellion's gathering place.

I nodded, turning my flashlight back on and following him. The dining hall was dark, but Stephen obviously knew his way around. He handed me a small wooden chest of tea bags while he boiled water over the stove. I chose a chamomile tea; it smelled like the face wash my father used when I was a child.

Stephen poured the hot water into a slightly chipped white mug, and I dropped the tea bag in. The steam spilled into the air, dancing through the beam of light from my flashlight.

“Thank you,” I said, holding the warm cup between my hands. “You have all been so welcoming to me. Why?” I asked.

The old man turned off the stove and faced me, his expression serious.

"We have all been where you are, unsure of whether or not anything we know is true. Change is hard for everyone, even an old man like me," Stephen said, laughing softly at his own comment.

Stephen left the dining hall, leaving me to finish my tea with my own thoughts for company. The longer I thought about these people and what they believed in, the more I questioned my own life. These people had no reason to lie to me and nothing to gain from going against Nanotech. I drained my mug in silence, savoring the taste of dried herbs.

My eyes drooped as I walked back to my room. Stephen's insomnia trick seemed to be working. I fell into a deep sleep as soon as I reached my bed.

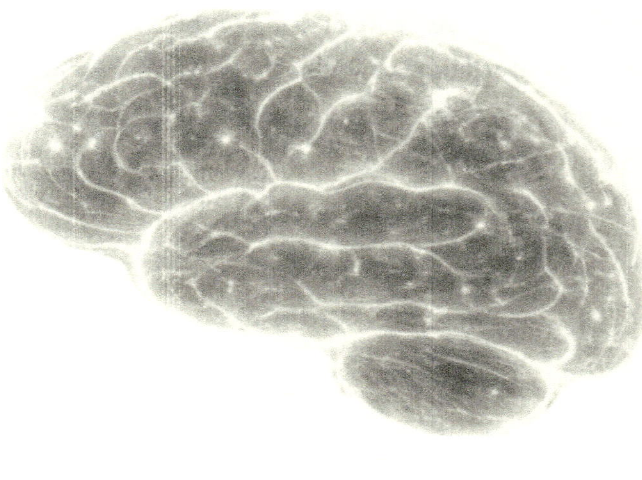

Chapter Ten

A Regular Family

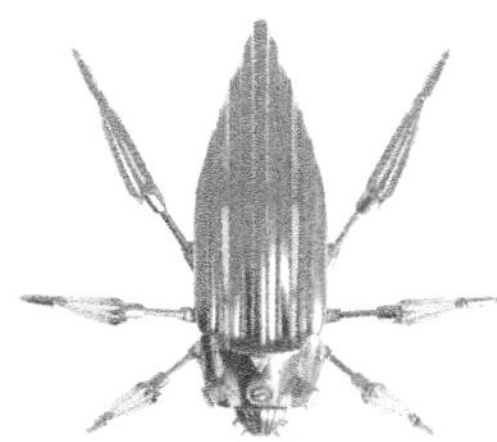

Trust was the first thing to break.

I woke to the sound of excited conversation. Warm light streamed under the door from the hallway. I pulled myself out of bed, brushing my hair from my neck. My clothes from yesterday were wrinkled and disheveled. I chose a set of one-size-fits-all clothes from the plastic tote and slipped them over my head. I could not say it was exactly one-size-fits-all, but they worked. The basic clothing looked strange with my shined shoes, but I stepped from my room without another thought. I did not really care how I looked around the others.

I found my way back to the dining hall with only one or two wrong turns and silently congratulated myself when I located the correct door. The voices grew louder as I got closer, and I was hit with a wall of sound when I pushed open the door. Everyone was gathered around the tables, some standing while others leaned over the benches, shoveling what I assumed was breakfast into their mouths.

I moved quietly to the stove, scraping the last bits of food from the saucepan into a plastic bowl. I found an empty spot at one end of one of the tables. I tried to decipher what everyone was talking about, but their voices blended together. I had never been great at understanding the dialects of Downtown Lin City, and everyone yelling did not help. I caught something about Mr. Anderson, but not much else.

Stephen sat quietly at the edge of the conversation, hovering and listening. I leaned toward him.

"What are they talking about?" I asked, taking a break from eating my breakfast.

Stephen shrugged. "Simon and Emmalyn are arguing about sending Adrien on missions, Adrien's talking about you getting your own room because he shared it with his brother, and Beatrice is mad that there was water next to the bathroom sink," he said.

I laughed. "Is it like this every morning?"

Stephen lowered his voice. "Yeah, but they'll tell you that they're just a regular family." He rolled his eyes.

I could not help but smile at the way Stephen spoke about the others. He seemed to be one of the oldest in the group, with grayed hair and wrinkles next to his eyes. His comments gave me the impression that he was a long-standing member of the alleged rebellion and had probably been dealing with people a third of his age for a while.

Adrien noticed my presence and stopped talking. He stared at me through his thick glasses with a sheepish smile, but the smile did not reach his eyes. Maybe his nature wanted to be joyful, but his situation did not allow it. I was still getting to know this group.

"It's nothing against you, Macie," he said, returning to his seat at the bench.

"What's nothing?" I asked.

"The room thing. It's just that we don't have a ton of space, so . . . I don't really know."

I rolled my eyes. "I get it, Adrien. You're just jealous because everyone already likes me better than you."

A blush rose across Adrien's face, and he turned away. Beatrice laughed heartily at my joke, clearly forgetting about her anger over the shared bathroom. I had always felt pride in my ability to make people forget their problems when I was younger. I guessed I still had that skill, but there was not much reason to use it in Uptown. Everyone there seemed to have no worries, or at least they kept their problems to themselves.

Beatrice, once she finished laughing, spoke in a friendly voice.

"Good morning, Macie. Did you sleep well?" she asked.

"Yeah," I said, giving a sideways glance to Stephen. "Everything was comfortable."

Beatrice nodded, apparently satisfied with my answer. I did not know if others were aware of Stephen's late-night tea brewing, but I thought it was safest not to mention more than I needed to. I was not able to gauge the actual trust between members of this so-called "family." I did not know what would cause arguments and what would bring us closer. I might have been overthinking everything, but that was how I managed to keep my place in Nanotech for the past few months, so I saw no reason to change tactics in this other collective.

Dr. Bethel entered the room, and the last conversations dwindled to only a couple of whispers. She raised her hand in greeting, and almost everyone else returned the gesture. I was not familiar with many of the signals and gestures used in Downtown, but they did not seem too complicated. I copied the movement.

The hushed conversations continued as Dr. Bethel stood at the head of the table.

"Good morning, everyone," she said.

Others responded with calm greetings. I marveled at the control Dr. Bethel had over the rowdy group sitting around her.

"I would like to see Macie, Emmalyn, and Adrien in my office," Dr. Bethel instructed.

The doctor walked back out of the room, Emmalyn close behind. I glanced at Adrien nervously before following Dr. Bethel, leaving the dining hall in a storm of whispering voices and speculation.

Dr. Bethel was already sitting behind the large white desk in her office when Adrien and I arrived. Her office was similar in size to the conference room I had been in the day before, but this space was much more comfortable.

Picture frames decorated the walls, some with photographs of people in the rebellion, others holding printed copies of headlines from weekly news programs. I had no idea how Dr. Bethel was able to print so many photographs on what looked like real paper. I was not able to focus on the pictures for very long before Emmalyn waved us toward the desk.

Adrien gave her his full attention. His feet were shoulder-width apart, and his hands were clasped behind his back as he waited for Bethel to speak. I copied his stance and leveled my eyes with Emmalyn's. Dr. Bethel spoke with authority.

"As you know, Macie, you have been offered a spot in the Lin City underground, our cause. Though I am not asking you for a final answer yet, Emmalyn and I have come up with something that may help you make that decision."

I nodded, silently waiting for Dr. Bethel to continue. I felt Adrien shift uncomfortably next to me. Neither of us knew why he was there yet. Dr. Bethel continued.

"We want you to travel back to Uptown, with Emmalyn as a chaperone, and plant a listening device somewhere in Ellis Anderson's private office."

I was stunned. How could someone I barely knew ask me to commit a crime against my own employer? Adrien spoke, clearly bothered by his lack of involvement.

"And what is it you want me to do?" he asked.

Dr. Bethel nodded at Emmalyn, giving her the floor.

"Aside from providing the recording device used for Anderson's office, we want you to figure out a way that Macie can use her communication devices to contact headquarters without being caught by monitors in Uptown," Emmalyn said.

Now it was Adrien's turn to be stunned.

"It's almost impossible to get anything through the blocks on Uptown devices, and you want me to give her a constant opening?" he asked incredulously.

Dr. Bethel smiled, revealing a yellowed set of teeth. Judging by her accent, she had lived her life in Downtown Lin City. Maybe that accounted for her impossible ideas.

Emmalyn spoke again, this time to me. "Unfortunately, Macie, we don't have the luxury of time to wait for your decision. We hope that, by using a recording device in Ellis Anderson's office, we can show you that he is, without the shadow of a doubt, the one behind all of this evil in Lin City."

Emmalyn was, of course, using the word evil to reference what Adrien had shown me the day before. The pictures and documents I had seen could have been easily altered to look like whatever Dr. Bethel wanted them to. Maybe I should go along with this plan to listen in on Mr. Anderson's day, to prove to myself–and everyone here–that nothing was going on. But if I was caught, I would never work in Lin City again. I might even be imprisoned on Level One.

"I'll do it."

The words surprised me as soon as I said them. What was I doing? This was not right, and I knew it. Bethel and Emmalyn exchanged a glance before turning back to me.

"Wonderful," Dr. Bethel said. "We'll get everything ready right away."

Chapter Eleven

The Bug

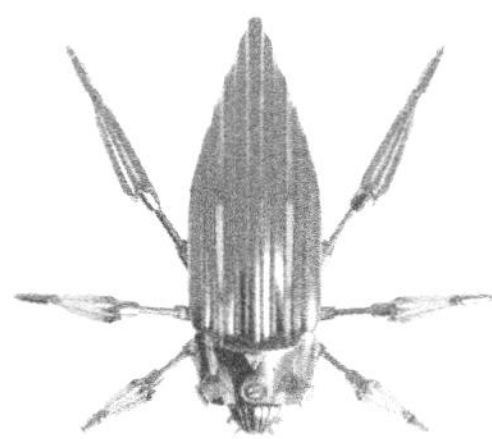

Some files aren't meant to be opened.

Emmalyn and I walked in silence as we climbed the levels of Lin City. levels of Lin City. She'd removed my blindfold when we'd climbed to Level Six, and with that, I realized that all I knew of the underground headquarters was that it was somewhere on Level Five. It was still very early in the morning. The only sounds that bounced around Midtown came from parents getting their kids ready for school or assembly-line employees leaving for an early shift. Light from apartments and multi-family housing units flowed into the streets so brightly that it almost hid the blue streetlights. Almost.

Michael had tossed my suit in with the general laundry while I was meeting with Bethel early that morning, so now I smelled like generic detergent and recycled water. I had not realized that the water conservation acts could monitor and control something as simple as washing machines. In Uptown, we did not think too hard about our personal water consumption. There were only laws for companies like Nanotech to follow.

"You know, I grew up on Level Nine," Emmalyn said, breaking her stoic silence.

"Really?" I asked.

I had assumed that everyone in the rebellion was from the lower levels. Not many people this high up had any issues with Nanotech. Not that I knew of, at least.

"I lived with my aunt, a sub-manager for the accounting sector. Until her accident, we lived within the circle of Nanotech."

I nodded. It was hard to tell what had prompted this discussion, but I was not going to stop her. Anything I could learn would be helpful.

"Dr. Bethel took me in after the accident. I've been with the rebellion ever since."

Part of me wanted to ask more about Emmalyn's aunt and her accident, but I knew prying would only get me back to square one with her.

I caught a glimpse of the rising sun as we reached the entrance to Uptown. Emmalyn turned from the path toward the gate and pulled me behind a concrete wall with unnecessary force.

"I can't get past the entrance with my ID. Take the recording device, drop it in Anderson's office, and retrieve it at the end of the day. You will return to headquarters alone. Understood?" Emmalyn asked.

Her voice was steely and hard, not like it had been on Level Five. She had been comfortable down there, surrounded by familiar people and places. I nodded, taking the small black recording device from her outstretched hand. Most of the device was plastic, but the metal switch on its base was cold against my palm.

"I'll be back as soon as I can," I said.

I rolled the device between my pointer finger and thumb and considered the depth of what I had agreed to do. I secretly hoped that nothing would come of this mission and that everyone who had been convinced by Dr. Bethel would realize the error of what she had told them.

Or . . . everything was true.

And that would mean everything I had been taught about my life was wrong. Either way, it did not seem like any of the people I had met over the past few days would be leaving anytime soon. I might as well do this one thing for them.

I walked out of the alleyway. The recording device was stowed in my breast pocket as I approached the gate to Uptown. Emmalyn's stare pressed against the back of my skull as I walked, but I refused to turn back. Any glance in her direction could alert the guards to her location, where she stood watching the gates–and me–intently.

The white gates were just as pristine as I remembered them, and I marveled at the view of the rising sun above them as I joined the queue of people waiting to enter Uptown. The line shuffled forward as people presented their ID badges to the guards and were either ushered through the cement gates or turned away. Those who were turned away never made a scene, but quietly made their way back into Midtown. I did not know why they were trying to get in if they did not have clearance. They must have had a reason.

I finally made it to the front of the line and produced my ID badge to the guard standing to the right of the gate. I had a moment of doubt, thinking that the recording device in my pocket would somehow be detected, but the light next to the gate flashed green, and I stepped through.

My hands were shaking as I returned my ID badge to my briefcase. I steadied my breath and walked into Level Ten.

The sound of wind filled my ears as I climbed the steps, pushing away the echo of shoes against metal that rose from Midtown. The regular chill of Uptown settled into my skin; it was strangely comforting in the early light. I averted my eyes as I approached the Nanotech tower. The sun reflected off the building's glass walls, cutting through my vision like knives. I scanned the chip in my arm on the panel next to the doors, and they slid open. I was nearly blinded as reflections danced across the glass.

Robby stood behind the receptionist desk and lifted his head as I entered.

"Good morning, Ms. Carson. I see that you're here all day. Would you like lunch sent to your office this afternoon?" he asked.

I shook my head, "No, I'll plan to meet you in the meal hall for a quick bite if I can."

Robby nodded before returning to his data screen. I walked quickly past the lobby, trying to avoid the overwhelming scent of roses that followed me around the main floor. I still had no idea how they got so many fresh roses. I could only assume that there were massive cold storage units somewhere filled with perfectly preserved flowers.

I opened my office door, sighing as the sun-filled air met my skin. My office seemed like one of the few places in Lin City where one could both see the sun and feel its warmth. I pulled the recording device from my pocket, watching as the black metal caught the light.

I walked the length of my office. My steps were slow, deliberate. I approached the door beyond my desk. I could not tell if Mr. Anderson was behind it or not. I pressed my ear against the cold surface; it had not yet been warmed by the sun. My pulse thudded in my ears. If this failed, it would not just be my job. It would be everything.

There was only silence.

Placing my free hand on the door, I slid it open manually.

A breath slipped through my teeth as I looked inside. There was no one there. I stood in the doorway for a moment, thoughts racing.

What am I doing? This is crazy. I'm crazy.

I stepped into the room. The plush carpet threw me off balance in my heeled shoes, and I steadied myself on the edge of Mr. Anderson's desk as a sharp pain flared through my ankle. The room was in its usual state of precision, with datapads and physical books arranged neatly along one wall. Mr. Anderson had the largest collection of physical books I had ever seen.

I moved toward the shelves and ran my fingers along the aged spines, then pulled back as I remembered the recording device still in my hand. The rest of the office was relatively bare, but his desk was a statement piece. It had been imported from the Rang Provinces, though I did not know by whom.

I crouched in front of the desk and used an adhesive tab to secure the device to the underside of the wooden panel.

I wanted to stay longer, to check every angle, to make sure the recorder was hidden, but there was no time. The doorway pulled me back toward my own office. I slid Mr. Anderson's door closed behind me and locked it.

My office was silent. The only sound was my heartbeat, rapid and uneven against my ribs.

It was another half hour before Mr. Anderson arrived, and I nearly jumped out of my skin when he opened the door. He raised his hand in greeting.

"Good morning, Macie. I didn't mean to startle you."

I nodded, forcing a sheepish smile.

"When you have a moment, please meet me in my office."

I faltered. What did he know?

Mr. Anderson walked past me, unalarmed by the startled look I had given him. I turned back to my monitor when I heard the door close softly behind him. I quickly retrieved an empty folder from my desk and scrawled a note before shoving it into my bag.

I have placed a recording device in Mr. Anderson's office. Return it and my things to Level Five. It may be necessary for the survival of the people of Lin City.

My hand shook as I zipped my bag closed. I still did not know if I believed Dr. Bethel's claims, but something in me had enough doubt to leave the note, just in case.

My jacket was disheveled when I stood, and I tugged it straight before turning toward Mr. Anderson's office. The door had been left unlocked. I only needed to slide it open. My hands were still shaking as I stepped inside.

Mr. Anderson had already set his things on his desk, and he motioned for me to sit. He looked like someone who should have been wearing glasses. Not because he was too old to see without them, but because his eyes seemed to bore into anyone in front of him. His gaze felt calculated. A layer of glass between his stare and me would have been welcome.

Without breaking eye contact, he spoke. "Macie, I noticed that you didn't return yesterday afternoon. I do you that you're feeling well. I pulled your records and noticed that you haven't been receiving your recommended nanobot boosters. Many people think injections are a one-time thing, but I recommend my employees receive one every month, depending on general health."

I stared at him as my mind buzzed. Why was he asking about this now?

"I'm only mentioning this because you have been doing a very fine job otherwise, and I want you to continue doing so," he said.

I could not speak. He had no idea about the people on Level Five or the recording device beneath his desk. I nodded.

Mr. Anderson took my silence as confirmation and excused me from the room.

“Macie,” he added before I reached the door.

I turned.

“Trust,” he said, not looking at me, “is the most fragile system we maintain here.”

Then he waved me out.

I scurried out quickly, exhaling as I felt the door click against my back.

Chapter Twelve

Keeping A Secret

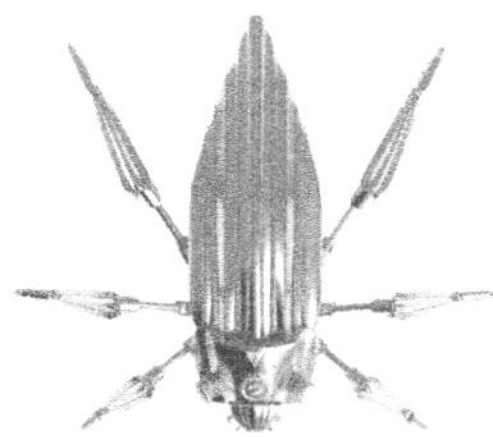

Something inside me was changing.

My office felt warmer than usual as I worked, and my stress sweat did not make that better. I tried to calm myself with monotonous tasks: answering messages, reviewing Mr. Anderson's schedule. Nothing worked. I did not even understand why I had done what I had. There was just something inside me that needed to know the truth. I was startled from my thoughts by a knock at my door. Do day nightmares exist? If they do, that would be more accurate. Tasha's voice pushed through the door, muffled but still recognizable.

"Macie, are you in here? Robby got us a table by the windows at lunch!"

With the peppiest voice I could muster, I responded, "Yup, just a second!"

I turned off my monitor and pushed back from my desk. Lunch would be good. It would distract me from everything else. Hopefully. Tasha waited in the hallway, a datapad tucked under one arm. Her expression was relaxed.

"Hey, Tasha. Let's head down."

The cafeteria was busier than usual. Everyone got excited for tacos–fake meat, of course. It was considered almost barbaric to eat animal meat in Lin City. I guessed that did not really apply Downtown, though. Tasha and I squeezed through the crowd and found Robby at a table near a wall of glass. The sun was almost directly overhead, so we had no trouble viewing the rest of Lin City.

Being with Tasha and Robby helped ease my anxiety, at least a little. They spoke as if everything here made sense, like the system really worked. Then they transitioned smoothly into office talk. They joked about what to get Doug for his upcoming retirement–something funny or something sincere? What kind of things did he even like? Everything they said went in one ear and out the other. I could not stop thinking about what would happen if they found out about the device. They had only known me for a few months. There was no way they could back me up. I did not want anything bad to happen to them if I was caught. I would have to trust them to do the right thing and pretend they had never known me.

Lunch always felt like the shortest part of my day, and I was back behind my desk before I knew it. The Nanotech schedule was strict, no matter your position. Work started at 7:30, lunch at noon, and we could leave at 4:00, but the building did not close in Uptown. I stayed as long as Mr. Anderson did. Until that day.

Mr. Anderson left the building at 5:30. I watched from my office window to make sure he was gone before I moved. I opened the door to his office quickly and dropped to the ground, running my hands along the underside of the desk. There was nothing there. My hands shook as they moved across the fine wood grain. This could not be happening. I could not have done this to myself.

I pressed my cheek against the floor, trying to catch a glimpse of the device. Something dug into my skin as I shifted, and I pulled back sharply. The recorder had fallen into the carpet, tangled among the thick fibers. I slipped the device into my pocket and stood, forcing myself to breathe steadily as I felt it between my fingers. I smoothed the carpet where I had knelt and hurried out. The door clicked behind me. I had done it.

It was hard not to break into a run on the way back to my apartment. I was eager to contact the rebellion, though I did not fully understand why.

Evening light streamed through the windows in my apartment when I arrived. I removed the communicator Dr. Bethel and Adrien had given me from the inner pocket of my briefcase. It was not fragile, but I still felt like it might crumble in my hands. It was such an antiquated device. It belonged in a display case, not in my apartment.

I hesitated before sending the signal they had taught me. I could just keep the communicator to myself. Would anything change if I never saw them again?

I sent the signal.

Without waiting for a response, I placed the communicator in a cabinet above my front door. The events of the day replayed in my mind as I ate my dinner. This was no longer the first step into my new life. I had already taken it, and there was no going back. Nothing would ever be the same.

Chapter Thirteen

Macie's Return

Nothing here existed without purpose.

I crawled into bed earlier than usual. Perhaps if I slept, time would pass more quickly. I wrapped myself in the warm comforter and stared out the window across from me.

I drifted in and out of sleep for hours. I could only tell that it was still night because of the faint blue hue filtering up from below. Eventually, I dragged myself from my bed before the sun had even risen. It did not feel like I had slept at all. My body felt heavy as I walked across my apartment and rubbed my hands on my dry cheeks. My skin still had not gotten used to the Uptown air.

I had not taken my hair down the night before, and my usually slick bun had been pushed to one side by my pillow. I pulled the pins and elastics from my hair. I did not have the energy to find a comb. Strands of hair stuck to the pins, and the prickling pain shook off any sleep left behind my eyes. I let my hair fall to my shoulders, not bothering to return it to its usual pristine condition.

The nutrient bars that typically filled my kitchen cabinets were running low, and I made a mental note to visit the grocer before the day was out. I appreciated the bar's predictable taste. They were not like the abnormally soft canned food I had eaten in Downtown. It was comforting to eat a warm meal, though, no matter how pureed it was.

Before I left, I remembered the communicator stowed above my door. The yellow indicator light above the number pad blinked rapidly. They had received my signal. The small screen displayed a message, one I could barely make out: an address. This must be the address of the building I had been in yesterday morning. They wanted me to know where it was, to go back. I decided that I would do that tonight. I would at least see if anything was on the recorder. If I did not go, everything I had done was for nothing.

My bag was still packed from the previous day, so I slung it over my shoulder and walked out the door. It took me getting to the front entrance of my apartment building before I realized that I had no idea where I was going. Work would not start for a few hours, and nothing was open. Nothing, except for the employee gym.

I drifted on my back in the calm water of the lap pool, letting my hair float around me. The smell of chlorine seemed to quiet my mind, making everything seem clearer. I had missed this. I focused on the rhythm of my breathing, each inhale steady, each exhale cutting clean through the water.

When I was in high school, I was the highest-awarded swimmer in Lin City. Swimming and competing had been my whole life. I was on track to compete on the world stage, or in the world pool at least. Then, it was all over. The reach for the final wall in the championship dislocated my should. It's never been the same.

I was interrupted from my thoughts when someone dove into the lane next to me. Water splashed, a few drops hitting my skin. I rolled my eyes. I loved being in the water, but I hated getting splashed. I had been pushed in the pool at more than one competition in school, and I could not stand it.

I swam to the pool stairs, grabbing my towel from the handrail. I felt better than I had in weeks, and I knew exactly what I wanted to do with the rebellion.

The workday slid by slowly. I spent hours in the cafeteria, directing the hanging of streamers and plastic banners for Doug's retirement party. Blue balloons floated through the air and bumped into light fixtures as they were pulled into position. The usually bland cafeteria looked slightly more exciting when I was done. Slightly.

In all the exceitement, I had forgotten to order a cake for Doug's retirement. Thankfully, someone in the resistance—probably Beatrice—had my back and it sat on the lunch table. It had white icing and a printed picture of Doug's face with the words "Congratulations Doug" above it. It felt strange, putting together a party after what had happened the last couple of days. If the stories from Downtown were true, why would Nanotech let people retire at all?

The department Doug was leaving was the first to arrive. Most of the employees came in bearing gifts and cards, well wishes for their colleague. I watched their smiling faces and wondered if they knew something, if they had seen the mangled bodies of supposed test subjects. How could someone live so blissfully if they had known darkness like that?

Tasha arrived with another group of communication agents from the connections department. She smiled when she saw me, but I did not acknowledge her. I felt bad, but maybe I could just pretend I was too focused on monitoring the party. That was not true, of course. I was completely consumed with reviewing the route to the Downtown building in my mind.

I left at the earliest possible moment, not bothering to say goodbye to anyone still at the party. They were all busy waiting in line for cake and showering Doug with compliments. Maybe he deserved all of this praise, or maybe he was hiding a secret bigger than this city could handle.

It was easy to get out of Uptown undetected. The guards did not really care who left. They only cared about who was trying to get in. When I was younger, I did not know why it was so hard to get into Uptown. Now I understood. It was for our safety, or maybe to hide the truth.

Midtown felt different in the evening. The streetlights buzzed over the trickle of Nanotech employees returning home late from work, their eyes tired and their faces sagging. I was sure they had started work before me, and they finished later, but that was just how life was in Lin City. If you made it to Uptown, you had earned your place there. Everyone knew that.

I adjusted the face covering I had donned in Uptown to avoid being recognized by any of the lower level employees. I was worried they may have seen me in the weekly enrichment programs standing next to Mr. Anderson.

There were posters plastered everywhere for the Downtown mayoral election. Some featured the face of Stephen Marshall, and others showed Teresa McKellen. McKellen was the incumbent mayor and lived in Uptown. Who better to make decisions for the people of Downtown than someone who did not have the stress of living there? I had not known Stephen before the other night. I did not really pay attention to Downtown politics. If such an obvious public figure believed in Dr. Bethel and everyone else in the rebellion, maybe it was true. Or maybe they recruited him to get as many people on board as possible. I would find out tonight.

I walked through a maze of multi-family units and convenience stores before finding the address I had been sent. Apparently, the maps provided by Nanotech were not completely up to date. Dozens of the businesses described in the legend were now nothing more than boarded-up concrete corpses. The building I arrived at was large but unassuming. The map indicated that it had once been offices for travel agencies. I recognized the name from when my grandparents told me how they used to leave the city all the time. Hardly anyone travelled now; where could you visit that would be better than Lin City?

Chapter Fourteen

Listening In

The patterns were always there.

Noise from the abandoned office building spilled out onto the street; laughter and voices bounced against walls and railings. I adjusted my jacket, flattened the frizz in my hair, and knocked on the front door. The voices inside lulled for a moment, and I heard footsteps approaching the other side of the door.

The door slid open with a harsh scrape, and Emmalyn's face greeted me, as stern and emotionless as when I had met her.

"Macie," Emmalyn said, scanning the catwalk behind me.

I had not even thought to make sure no one was following me on the way down.

"Come in."

I slipped past Emmalyn as she pulled back the door, letting the soft fluorescent lights fill my vision. I was thankful for the yellow-tinted illumination inside; those blue bulbs were giving me a migraine.

Many of the people I had met two days ago were lounging around the front room in plastic chairs with uneven legs. They rocked back and forth slightly as they spoke, making it look like everyone was trying to stay balanced on a boat in rough waters. Everyone quieted when I entered.

Dr. Bethel stood from her chair and walked toward me, extending her hand, palm up. After fishing around in my pocket for a moment, I produced the recorder. She nodded.

"Thank you, Macie. I am so glad you decided to join us," she said, a smile creeping into the creases around her eyes.

I frowned. "I haven't decided anything for sure yet."

My voice was harsher than I intended, but I spoke only the truth.

Dr. Bethel handed the recorder to Adrien, who inspected the device carefully.

"You'll stay for the same reason I'm still here," she said confidently.

Dr. Bethel's voice was comforting, but her words startled me. She did not know me at all, and she did not know what I had decided.

Simon spoke to Emmalyn, quietly enough to look like he was hiding it, but loud enough that everyone could hear.

"Did anyone follow her here?"

Emmalyn shook her head. She began to speak, but looked at me and decided against it. I guessed I would not find out every truth that night.

Adrien, after a thorough inspection of the recording device, waved me over.

"We will go to the server lab and take a look at this recording. Matthew," he pointed at a man sitting next to Emmalyn, "will join us and research anything we hear come up. Think of him as a fact checker," he finished.

Matthew got up and joined us in the center of the room. After a short introduction, and a nod from Simon and Emmalyn, I followed Adrien and Matthew from the foyer. Conversation resumed behind us.

I recalled the halls of the rebellion's headquarters seemed barren the first time I had been there, but now, on my second pass, I could see they were dotted with pictures and handmade decorations, some of which were obviously done by children. Adrien's office had been left unlocked, and the three of us entered quietly. The room was dark and cramped once the door had been closed again. There was an air recycler in one corner, presumably to help keep moisture away from the computers, and a neatly made bed on the wall opposite the monitors. I realized that this room was probably not only the surveillance center for the entire rebellion, but also Adrien's bedroom. I could not imagine living without basic privacy. I had not even liked the idea of a roommate for an apartment when I moved out of my parents' place. I was grateful to be on my own.

Adrien turned on one of the large computers beneath his desk and sat in a rolling office chair, swaying side to side as we waited for the monitors to light up. Matthew took a seat on the end of Adrien's bed, and I opted to remain standing. I did not even know these people, and I did not really want to get to know them. A few of the monitors in front of me suddenly flashed white, shocking me out of whatever thoughts had been occupying my mind.

Adrien copied the data from the recording device onto the computer and began playing it. His hands moved quickly and precisely, like someone who knew there would be no second chances if mistakes were made. He switched to a visual representation of the recording that made it easy to identify the brief periods of conversation amongst the hours of silence. Matthew thanked him. Matthew thanked him.

We skimmed through my meeting with Mr. Anderson and returned to normal speed when we heard the ringing of his datapad. Mr. Anderson always wore an earpiece, so we did not hear anything from the caller, but what he said was more than a little strange to Adrien and Matthew.

"Yes, this is him."

Pause.

"Oh, of course. Yes, my team has been looking forward to hearing from you."

More pauses followed each time he waited for the other person to speak.

"In a few days," he paused. "Can you hide it this close?"

A moment of silence.

"Yes, that should work. What have you heard so far about the project?"

"I see. Good. I will send someone to meet you then. Great working with you."

Then, a beeping sound.

Adrien paused the recording when Mr. Anderson terminated the call, and we all sat in silence.

"Why hadn't you heard about a meeting coming up, or a new project?" Adrien asked, looking suspicious.

"Isn't it usually your job to take calls and schedule face-to-face meetings?" Matthew added.

"You mean, why do I think this caller connected straight to his office instead?" I asked.

Matthew and Adrien were clearly looking for an answer from me. Finally, I spoke.

"It is likely that he already knew the caller. I have heard rumors about a secret code that callers can give to be connected straight to any employee, regardless of status in Nanotech. I haven't been able to confirm whether it is true with anyone of importance, though."

Adrien listened quietly and fiddled with his glasses as he thought.

"That would be awfully irregular for a high-profile employee. Maybe it's more like an approved list, where certain people can give their city identification number to gain access?"

Adrien's statement was half a question, but I could not give a real answer.

"All calls have to go through the main switchboard before they can get to me or Mr. Anderson. They would know every person who called, which would not be very secretive," I responded.

Matthew typed something into his datapad. I wished I had spent more time learning how to read upside down in school. After a few more seconds of quiet thought, Adrien unpaused the recording.

We sat in that small, dark room for hours, replaying every creak of Mr. Anderson's chair and listening to the tapping of Matthew's fingertips on his datapad. In moments of silence in the recording, Adrien and I made small talk.

We talked about our time in school and what shows we watched during weekly enrichment programs. Both of us were longtime fans of the science fiction drama *Kit River*, about a team of the smartest people in the world who were chosen to band together on a space expedition. It had been going on for almost seven years, with multiple recasts and characters killed off because their actors were difficult to work with. We debated our favorite episodes until the small hours of the morning.

The recording ended with the sound of me sifting through the carpet. Matthew suggested I hide it near hardwood next time. I did not find this amusing.

The phone call had not been completely damning on its own, but a quick look at Mr. Anderson's calendar solidified the conspiracies in my mind. The call had been completely unscheduled, and two days from now was completely blocked off, with no title given to the event.

Adrien accompanied me to my room, though I had already learned the halls well enough to find it myself. We parted ways without much speaking, but as I entered the room, I found fresh clothes on my bed, closer to my size, and a warm cup of tea on my tote bin.

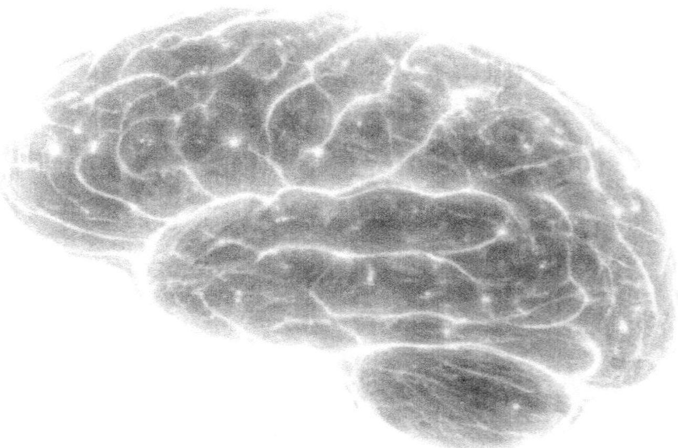

Chapter Fifteen

The Briefing

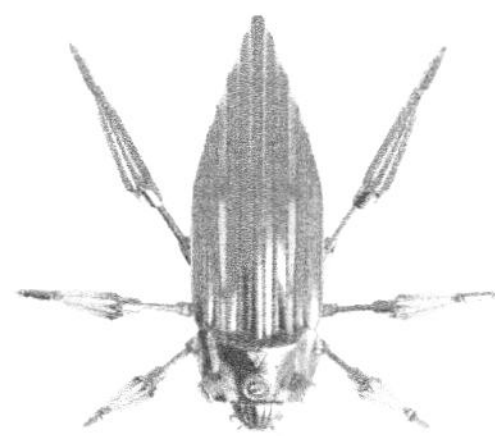

They controlled more than they admitted.

Someone knocked on my door early in the morning, startling me from a dream about swimming with dolphins. I had never seen one, but I had seen pictures. After remembering where I was, I moved to the door. There was no peephole or view screen to the hallway, so I opened the door a crack. Stephen was on the other side, impatiently tapping his foot.

He huffed sarcastically when he saw me. "They sent me to get you for breakfast. Hurry up so we can get it hot!"

I quickly slipped my feet into the shoes that had been left by the door the night before and joined Stephen in the hall. I began to piece together a map of the rebellion's building and made my way to the dining room with little trouble, even if Stephen had not been with me. Impressing Stephen made me feel like I had gotten a good grade in math. Why was I even looking for validation from any of them, people I did not even trust?

The dining hall was illuminated by lanterns from the brand Sunny Day. It claimed to give users the same benefits as the real sun. Now that I was living in the gaze of the real sun, I found it hard to believe that something artificial could even come close. I was welcomed to the meal with smiles and waves, not familiar, but still kind. A seat next to Dr. Bethel had been left open for me, and Emmalyn sat on the doctor's other side. The meal that day was more solid than the soup I had tried before. It consisted of baked beans, from the can, of course, and a sort of mashed animal egg I was not familiar with. Dr. Bethel informed me that it was a synthesized version of a chicken egg, though its green tint was unsettling.

"Macie here is incredible at learning a new place," Stephen said. "She practically led me here this morning!"

I shrugged, trying to seem humble. "I've always memorized maps for fun. I liked being the only fifth-year student who knew every road in Uptown, although none of us had been there."

Bethel nodded thoughtfully as the plates were taken away to be cleaned.

"Macie, that might actually be perfect for where I'm sending Simon and Stephen tomorrow. We are trying to get a look at a trade happening on Level Four then, but I can't have either of them stopping to make sure they're going the right way. Your skills would be perfect."

The entire room was looking at me now, some with kindness in their eyes, others with skepticism. Before I knew what I was saying, I agreed. Like an idiot.

Once the dishes were clean and most people had cleared from the dining hall, I was given a datapad with the maps of Level

Four pulled up. I already knew the more traveled parts of the level pretty well, but the back alleys we would be dealing with that day were completely new.

I stayed in the dining hall as I reviewed the maps. The room not only sported faux sunlight, but the vents above and around the stovetop provided a source of ventilation not present in other areas. I overlaid the map of the back alleys onto the map I already had, referencing landmarks and street names I already knew.

Emmalyn joined me after about an hour by myself.

"Now that you're becoming part of this team, it's time for you to learn how to defend yourself." She said.

"I took one of those women's defense classes on a girls' trip to the Rang capital last year, that probably counts," I replied. I was only partly joking.

"Not quite what I'm looking for, but at least you have a basic understanding. Let me show you the training room."

Emmalyn led me from the dining hall, where I left my data-pads on the table, and to a part of headquarters I hadn't seen before. The training room was about the size of the entry hall, with foam mats on the floor and a variety of weapons lining the walls.

"Whoa, that's a lot of guns," I remarked, gesturing towards one wall.

"And this isn't even the armory," Emmalyn smirked.

I was led to one of the foam mats, and my training began. We started with basic skills, like maintaining balance and protecting your face. I could tell that Emmalyn did her best to hide a laugh whenever my body met the floor. After about the fifth time I faceplanted into the mats, I finally figured out how to keep my knees bent.

I pointed to a row of plastic poles on one rack.

"Wouldn't it be a bit fairer if I got one of those nice staffs, and you just had your hands?"

Emmalyn shook her head, "Nanotech won't make the fight fair, and neither will I."

We continued sparring until we were both out of breath, I much so more than her.

We returned to the dining hall and found Simon, looking over my datapads. He held a device with which I was not familiar.

“How’s it going, Macie?” he asked.

I did not want to engage in small talk with this man. I did not trust anyone who was willing to kidnap another person.

“What’s that?” I asked, gesturing to the device he held.

Simon set it on the table and pushed it toward me. The device was a disc made of shiny silver metal, probably aluminum. It featured an array of buttons on one of the flat sides, many of which were labeled with numbers or arrows. I picked it up and ran my fingers onto its smooth edges.

“It’s a healing device that is used in the provinces that can’t get nanobot shipments regularly. It’s usually used by medical professionals, but Bethel wanted you to have it, just in case.”

“My parents were super into all of this traditional medicine stuff. I think they used something similar when my brother broke his arm. Never quite healed right, though,” I said.

“Well, that’s why everyone uses nanobots if they can. Are your parents the reason you don’t get the injections?” Simon asked.

He seemed sincere, but I was in an unfamiliar place. Anything I said then could be used against me.

"It's a long story," I said.

The truth was, I could probably sum up the reason I never had injections in a couple of sentences, but he did not need to know anything about my past or my family.

Simon did not push it.

After a beat of silence, Simon stood from the table. "What do you think about joining a couple of us when we head out to get some groceries? We'll make sure to keep your face covered, like you did on the way down." His voice was kind, and I was interested in getting a better look at Downtown.

After another glance at the work in front of me, I joined Simon by the door. "Sure, maybe I can get a taste of more than canned stew."

Simon laughed at my remark. It would not be long before I learned that there were not many other options.

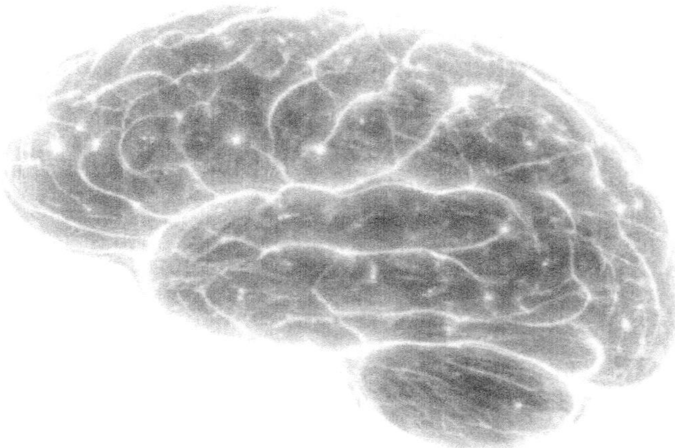

Chapter Sixteen

GRUB-MART

The evidence didn't start with me.

I missed the artificial sunlight as soon as we stepped out of the rebellion's headquarters. I was dressed in an outfit of gray and black, with a bulky jacket and a large scarf wrapped around my head and most of my face. My lack of color blended into the walls, and the jacket sported more pockets than I knew what to do with. I was not used to hiding.

Our shopping group consisted of Simon and Beatrice—Bea, she said I should call her. Bea did not live at headquarters, so she met us as we approached the store. She greeted me with a smile and a grocery list. The shop closest to headquarters was a compact Grub-Mart location, with floor-to-ceiling shelves completely stacked with canned vegetables, soups, stew, and fruit cocktail. Large empty water jugs sat by the front door, waiting to be refilled and resold. Sacks of dried food sat in the back of the store, seemingly untouched. I pointed to the abandoned food. It was mostly beans and rice, which I thought was better than chewy meat stew.

"Why don't we grab one of those bags? They're cheaper and will probably last longer?" I asked.

Beatrice shook her head, not even looking to the back of the store. "Water costs more than anything else in here. Canned food doesn't need any water to be ready, and you don't have to drink as much if your meal is forty percent water, anyway."

I nodded and continued through the racks of food with their straightforward labels. It was obvious that form over function was not a popular marketing tactic Downtown. Simon carried the reusable bags from headquarters, one on each arm filled with cans and a suspiciously cheap brand of bottled water. The total bill from Grub-Mart was more than I expected, but I had spent the past few months living on coffee and nutrient bars that shipped in bulk to my apartment each week. Bea grimaced as she paid the cashier. Feeding the number of mouths in headquarters was hard on anyone's salary. I learned later that the money was a collection from multiple people in the rebellion. Everything else went to keeping the AC and electrical running.

The lower you went in Lin City, the hotter it was. It was a shock to come down after being in Uptown, or at least the upper levels of Midtown, my whole life. Once we were done in Grub-Mart, I could already feel sweat dripping beneath my jacket. Most businesses could not justify the cost of internal cooling. I was grateful that Dr. Bethel did.

It was apparently lunchtime on Level Five when we left, and I was met with the faces of hundreds of Nanotech factory workers, all wearing the same off-white uniform. Half of the uniforms were stained with brown or black. I wondered why they even made them white if they were stained so easily. I asked Beatrice and Simon about it, not really caring which one answered.

Bea spoke first. “Workers have their pay docked if they show up with a dirty uniform. Making them white makes them almost impossible to clean.”

I was confused, but stayed silent. If it were impossible, why penalize the workers?

We weaved through the swarms of people, watching as they pulled half-full cans of food from their work bags. They all ate quickly, no matter the consistency of their lunch. The thought of the canned stew I had eaten being cold made my stomach churn.

Headquarters was lively when we returned. All the doors had been opened, and people milled in and out freely. Adrien greeted us, taking the food from his brother.

“The lines have never been this busy. We might have to shut Downtown early today,” he said, gesturing to the line that had formed outside of the front doors.

Apparently, I looked confused enough for Adrien to provide an explanation as we made our way inside.

“We started a soup kitchen here as a cover for the building’s true purpose. Nothing is very nutritious, but it’s better than starving.”

What I saw inside the foyer reminded me of images in old history books I had read in school. Lines of men and women filed to tables covered in pots and pans, being served an amalgamation of different canned soups and vegetables. A sour mix of heated metal, canned broth, and too many bodies clung to the air, thick enough to taste. I had always thought this way of life had ended when Nanotech arrived in Lin City. Whoever taught me that was obviously wrong. The people of Downtown needed the help of places like this just to survive, even though they were employed by Nanotech.

Chapter Seventeen

Into The Tunnels

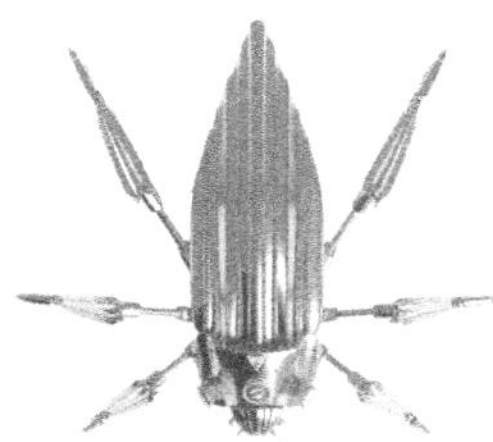

People didn't leave—they vanished.

I was woken early by the alarm I had set on my datapad. The clothes I had been given the night before were still neatly folded on the bin next to my bed, and I dressed quickly. It was a mostly black suit, with a utility vest and boots with thick tread on the soles. Almost every inch of my skin was covered, leaving only my fingertips exposed. I would need them to operate the communication device Adrien had for me.

My mind filled with doubt as I readied myself for the morning's journey. I had seen so much evidence in support of the rebellion, but a tiny voice in my mind still questioned what truth anything here held. Everything was still so new.

I reviewed the maps on the rebellion's datapad once more before leaving my room. The maps would be completely erased as soon as we left for the mission, so they could not be found if headquarters was attacked. This was obviously protocol for any serious outing the rebellion had. No one even batted an eye when Adrien told me that, because I had a chance of not coming back alive, I could not bring the datapad or any other information with me.

Simon and Matthew were already waiting in the foyer when I arrived. Adrien was there too, juggling three sets of earpieces and battery packs. He smiled when he saw me, but the other two only had faces of stony determination. This had always been life or death for them, and now it was for me, too.

Adrien adjusted the in-ear wires beneath my hood, making sure that nothing was visible from the outside. Surveillance in lower Downtown was tight. If the Lin City guards saw so much as a suspicious hoodie string, they had the right to search you.

Adrien's hands moved carefully through my hair, weaving the wire into my elastic like it was just another strand. I was relieved to see that the others were covered in the same thick, dark clothing. At least I would not be overheating alone.

The meeting with Bethel that followed was a blur. All I could hear was my own heartbeat rattling through my chest.

Level Five was still shadowed when we left headquarters, our black outfits blending into the darkness beneath the blue streetlights. I led Simon and Matthew through the maze of back alleys, forcing confidence into every turn. They trusted me enough to let me lead them. I had to make every decision seem calculated.

Matthew put a hand on my shoulder when we passed the entrance to Level Four. I could not tell how long we had been walking. There was no sunlight in Level Four, ever. Matthew pointed to a large trash compactor, and I followed him toward it. He crouched behind it, and Simon moved past us to stand in the shadows. He was barely visible from the mouth of the alley, with a better line of sight than either of us. We just had to hope no one looked too closely at the dark corner where he stood.

We waited in complete silence for what felt like hours. Even my breathing sounded too loud. People passed us on their way to work, completely unaware of what was happening right next to their front doors.

Eventually, they appeared.

Two figures walked into the alley where we hid, both holding datapads and muttering to each other under their breath. I saw Matthew tense beside me, subtly pointing to one of the pockets on my vest. Reaching inside, I pulled out a rectangular recording device. This one could pick up more than the one I had placed in Mr. Anderson's office, but it was also much larger. My first task seemed so long ago now. Everything had changed since then.

I pushed the slider on the side of the device and watched the light turn red when it started recording. Holding it out as far as I could, I covered the glow with my hand and edged it closer to the lip of the trash compactor. Though I trusted Adrien's expertise, I did not want to miss a thing.

The two figures stood alone for a few moments before they were joined by another. This person pushed a large metal cart, presumably the shipment mentioned in the call.

"Is this all of it?"

"Yes. Remember, follow the instructions carefully. All you're doing is storage. If anything goes missing...."

One of the first figures waved dismissively and handed the other a datapad.

"We know. Here. Everything is signed and ready to go."

There was a quick exchange before the cart changed hands. The deliverer left quickly, glancing over their shoulder before turning the corner. The other two spoke quietly for a moment and moved deeper into the alley. I held my breath as they approached the trash compactor. I turned toward Simon and Matthew. Both were still and silent. The camera on the front of Simon's vest had been partially covered in black tape, but I could see a faint reflection of blue light in its lens. I hoped I was the only one who noticed it.

The figures stopped in front of the wall beside my hiding spot and activated a panel I had not noticed before. A white number pad lit up, and after one of them entered a short code, part of the cement wall shifted aside.

My breath caught as I leaned against the trash compactor, trying to get a better view. The maps I had memorized had shown no exit from this alley.

The two figures, unfazed, began pushing the metal cart through the opening. Matthew put a hand on my shoulder, but I brushed him aside. Peering around the edge, I saw a long, damp hallway. The walls curved slightly, but the lights were what stood out. The ceiling was lined with rectangular fluorescent fixtures, and they were not blue.

I heard Matthew whisper sharply behind me, but I continued forward. The figures had turned away and were speaking freely. They would not notice if I slipped in behind them.

I crawled halfway into the opening. Matthew tried to pull me back, but he did not want to hurt me, and I shook him off. I glanced back at him, and he shook his head hard. Adrien's voice came through my earpiece.

"Macie, whatever you're thinking about doing, don't–"

The earpiece came free easily. I tucked it under my collar.

My fingers tightened around the edge of the opening, my pulse hammering so hard it felt like it might give me away.

I hesitated for a fraction of a second, then moved fully into the tunnel. The entrance slid shut behind me with the scrape of stone on stone. The sound echoed longer than I expected.

For a moment, cut off, I heard nothing. No voices. No footsteps. No way back.

But I needed to know where the shipment was going. This was my mission, and I was going to finish it. This wasn't hesitation anymore. This was the choice.

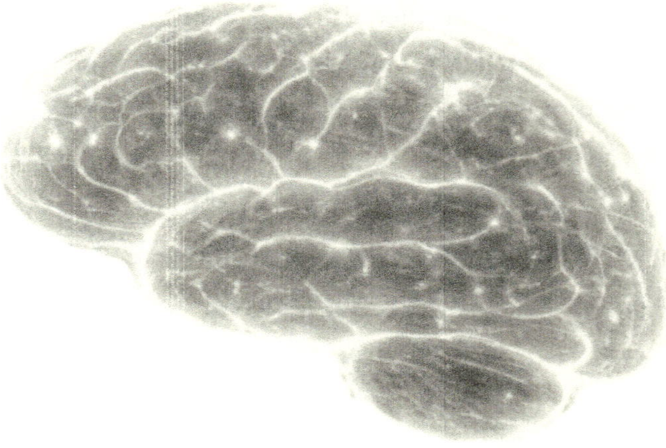

Chapter Eighteen

Macie Alone

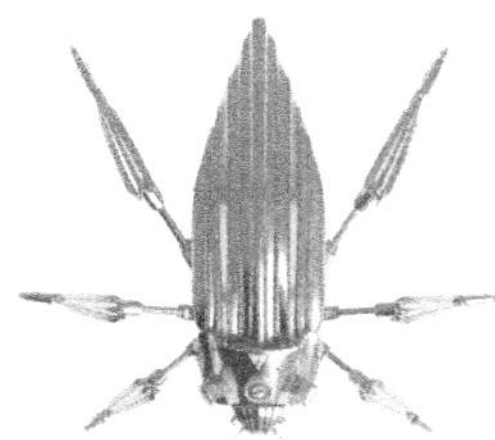

Every answer created a new doubt.

I got to my feet and looked around. There was a thin layer of grime and water on the ground, reflecting the dim light above. My black outfit did not camouflage me as well without the blue streetlights, so I dumped the vest and boots quietly. I would need to rely on stealth more than blending in.

The figures and their cargo had continued down the hall and were becoming difficult to see. I followed them carefully, avoiding puddles when I could. The sound of dripping pipes surrounded me. Where was I?

I took in every detail I could see, hoping to remember anything I could bring back to headquarters. The people in front of me did not look back. If they did, I would be dead.

Eventually, the figures reached a branch in the hallway. I followed them through the right passage. The hallway was similar in lighting and environment, but dotted with panels like the one that had first opened the wall in the alley. I assumed these opened into other parts of the city.

The pair stopped in front of one of the panels and entered something quickly. I was too far away to see if the code was the same as before, but the entrance opened in the same way. Bright light spilled into the damp hallway, and one of the figures exclaimed.

They continued through the new opening with the crate, and I approached quietly. The room was sterile and white, with rows of crates identical to the one being added. I still held the recording device in my palm, and after a brief inspection of the opening, I wedged it into a narrow gap between the wall and the nearest crate.

I could not see the figures anymore, but I could hear their voices drifting through the room. I could not risk following them. It would be far too easy for someone to spot me in an open storage space.

I jumped back into the hall as the door automatically closed with a deafening scrap. I stood in the hallway for a moment longer, taking in what I had seen. Adrenaline surged through me as I turned back the way I had come, trying to stay calm as I walked. My socks were slick with grime now.

I turned left at the intersection and saw the control panel where I had entered. My boots and vest were still shoved into one corner. I pulled them on quickly. Stepping up to the panel, I entered the code I had seen earlier. The entrance scraped open, and I stepped back into the alley. Simon and Matthew were gone. I should have known they would not wait, but it was still jarring not to see them there.

Headquarters was quiet when I arrived. Apparently, the food bank had already closed. I pressed the comm button beside the door and waited. It opened almost immediately, and I was pulled inside. Emmalyn had been waiting on the other side, and she was not pleased.

Her jaw tightened for just a moment before her expression smoothed back into control.

"What were you thinking?" she demanded, slamming the door closed behind me.

I yanked my arm away. "I was thinking I had an opportunity to finish the mission. Where is Dr. Bethel?"

"You weren't followed?" she asked, too quickly. Then, shaking her head, "She's on her way."

I tried to think of something intelligent to say, but Bethel and Adrien entered mid-conversation, both speaking quickly. Before they could redirect their attention to me, I spoke.

"I know I could have stayed with Simon and Matthew, but I needed to finish the mission. If you check the recording, you'll see it's still active, and I planted it where they put the shipment!"

Dr. Bethel nodded. "We know, Macie. You've been connected to comms the whole time."

I froze. I could not believe I had forgotten about the wires. Of course they could still hear everything.

"Where were you?" Adrien asked.

I shrugged. "I don't know. It was this long hallway that wasn't really a hallway, more like tunnels, and there was water everywhere. It was disgusting."

Bethel and Emmalyn exchanged a look.

"What you're describing sounds like the water reserve systems that used to store emergency supplies in case of drought," Emmalyn said. "They ran dry decades ago, and now they're being used for Nanotech's more secretive operations."

I nodded along, but it was difficult to process. The water reserves had been a point of pride when I was in school, and I had no idea they were empty. You would never know it in Uptown; we weren't required to ration it there.

After a series of rapid questions about the storage room and the other doors I had seen, Dr. Bethel pulled me aside.

"Macie, I'm worried you've been out of Uptown for too long," she said.

"Not at all. They just think I'm sick," I replied.

In truth, I just did not want to go back. Dr. Bethel sighed, clearly sensing my hesitation.

"Even so, they will eventually realize that someone with nanobot injections wouldn't still be sick. You need to go back and stay for at least a few days. We'll keep in touch the entire time."

I was disappointed, but I did not argue. I left before sunrise, dressed in my suit and heels, ready for another lie.

Chapter Nineteen

An Impromptu Interview

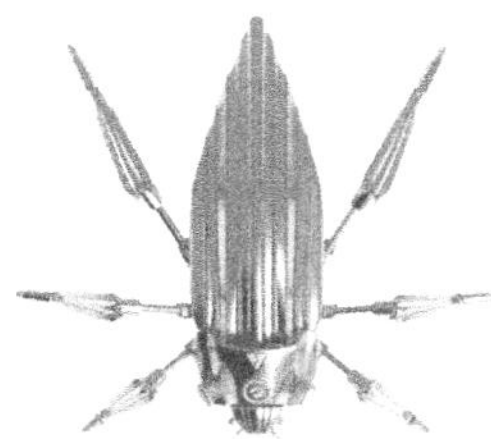

The truth came with consequences.

It was a few days before I noticed the new message from headquarters blinking on the communicator. It was Adrien. I had been messaging headquarters about a back elevator I had found in Nanotech and decided that Adrien and decided that he would join me after work, under the guise of a job interview, to collect as much data as possible from the lower levels of the Nanotech compound.

This would be my highest-risk mission yet. I was risking not only my career, but my life by investigating Nanotech itself. I was so focused on planning the mission that evening in my head that I nearly bumped into Tasha outside my apartment.

"Hey, Macie!" Tasha called, snapping me from my thoughts.

I looked at her, trying to bring some life into my eyes.

"Oh, sorry, Tasha. I've got a lot on my mind," I said, falling into step beside her.

"I get it. I know you've been getting sick a lot lately. Remember, if you need anything, I'm just next door," Tasha said, her voice full of sincerity.

"Thanks, I really appreciate it," I replied.

For a moment, I almost told her everything, but I stopped myself. Mr. Anderson was right about one thing. Trust was a fragile system. Now more than ever.

I always tried to be just as kind to Tasha as she was to me, but it had been hard to see her in the same way after joining the rebellion. I was sure she did not know half the things I did, but my empathy wavered more and more the longer I watched the people of Lin City suffer under Nanotech's control.

Tasha and I walked quietly through Level Twelve, the sound of our shoes bouncing off the buildings around us. Tasha looked as jubilant and confident as always. She gave off a kind of radi-ance that made you resent her when you understood what she really did for work. She was not just communicating for Nanotech; she was marketing the destruction of her own species.

When I reached my office, I entered quickly. I only acknowl-edged Tasha's goodbye with a nod.

I dropped my bag next to the desk and let my shoulders slump without the weight. I sat down, and my bright white screen welcomed me with an animation of a smiling sun. I did not know what time Mr. Anderson would arrive, but I had to make sure I was prepared for Adrien's arrival before he saw anything.

I started my preparations by calling the HR department through my earpiece. The ringing rattled through the tiny bones in my ear like rolling dice as I waited for them to pick up.

"Hello. This is Nanotech Incorporated Human Resources," the voice said.

The voice was androgynous and smooth. It reminded me of a teacher I once had in graduate school.

"Hi, this is Ms. Carson calling from Mr. Anderson's office. I would like to interview a potential intern after work today. He will need access to Level Ten and the Nanotech lobby."

I heard the clack of a datascreen keyboard before the voice responded. "Of course, Ms. Carson. I'll notify the reception desk right away. Would you like me to send a recording of this call to Mr. Anderson's office?"

"No!" I said.

There was a brief silence on the other end, and I cursed myself for the reaction. I could not afford to raise suspicion, especially not with the person allowing a member of the Lin City underground into the Nanotech complex.

The voice cleared their throat. "As you wish, Ms. Carson. Have a nice day."

My earpiece beeped as the call ended. I pulled the cord from my ear and dropped it onto my desk. The folders in front of me seemed to stare back, urging me to work, but I turned away. The sun had already crept above the horizon, its yellow light washing over me. I stood and walked toward the window as if in a trance.

I pressed my hands against the glass and felt the warmth of the morning light against my palms. When I closed my eyes, I remembered what it was like growing up on Level Nine. The only warmth I felt came from the space heaters around my home. Sometimes, in the winter, when I sat shivering in front of them, I imagined the sun beating down on me. Now I had the sun, and I was risking my life to make sure others could see it someday too.

I heard the lock click as someone unlocked the door with an ID badge, and I darted back to my desk, opening a folder in front of me. Mr. Anderson strode in, letting the door swing closed behind him.

He wore a gray suit with polished black shoes and a bright blue tie, the same color as his eyes. If I squinted, I could almost see the remnants of his old life. His hair was whiter than most men his age, and his left arm moved strangely at his side, as if he were more accustomed to using a cane.

Mr. Anderson greeted me with a nod and continued into his office. I heard the second door lock behind him. I exhaled slowly and looked back down at the folder in front of me. I had randomly selected a report about water usage at Nanotech. I had seen these reports before, but they disgusted me every time.

I had seen children unconscious from dehydration in Downtown, but people here had enough water to keep a dozen houseplants thriving. I copied the files into Mr. Anderson's system, my movements automatic. I could not stop checking the time every few minutes. The day could not end fast enough.

Mr. Anderson left after lunch, claiming he had a meeting with the head of Nanotech's medical units. I thought he was lying, though there was nothing I could do to prove it.

I did not meet Tasha or Robby in the lunch hall. I was too anxious to eat. Instead, I stayed in my office, memorizing as much information as I could. I had learned from Aria's story that writing anything down or taking pictures would get me caught before I could pass it along, so I relied on memory. No one could take that from me.

I was surprised when Tasha knocked on my door. The workday was finally over. I cracked the door open and forced a look of regret.

"Sorry, Tasha, I'm going to work late today," I said.

Tasha waved it off. "Don't worry about it. I'll see you tomorrow!"

I nodded and smiled, closing the door as she walked away. My expression fell the moment I turned back into the room. I watched my coworkers disperse into Uptown from my window, my forehead pressed against the cooling glass. They looked like pebbles, scattering through a maze of metal and cement.

Once the crowd thinned, I gathered my things and slung my bag over my shoulder. I left my office, the door locking behind me as it always did. My heart raced as I walked toward the lobby. I was surprised I could not see my ribcage trembling beneath my jacket.

Adrien was already there, sitting on a plush white couch. He wore a navy suit that I could tell had been handed down from Simon. His hair was combed back, and he wiped his glasses obsessively with the edge of his sleeve. He smiled when he saw me.

I waved to Robby, making sure they were watching as I extended my hand for Adrien to shake. He stood, holding one arm stiffly behind his back like he was at attention.

"Good evening, Mr. Davis. Please follow me to the conference room, and we can begin the interview."

Adrien nodded, and I turned on my heel, leading him toward one of the meeting rooms. When we reached the large doors labeled with a gold plaque reading Amber Chase Conference Room, I kept walking. I had instructed security not to disturb the interview, so no one should question our absence. I hoped.

I fought the urge to run as the elevator doors came into view. Adrien quickened his pace behind me, clearly just as eager as I was to begin the real mission and explore the unseen depths of the Nanotech complex. Or at least, depths from which no one had returned.

The control panel beside the elevator lit up as we approached. I called the elevator and waited in tense silence, hardly daring to breathe.

We waited in silence. The only sound in my ears was the rush of my own blood as my body braced for danger. The elevator chimed, and I flinched. Adrien tried to hide a laugh behind me.

The doors slid open, and we stepped inside.

The interior was large enough for at least a dozen people, with hooks along the walls for cargo. The floors and walls were made of scratched metal, and everything carried a faint, earthy smell. The doors shut behind us with a sharp squeak.

Adrien relaxed slightly once they closed. After a moment of silence, he handed me a comm device from headquarters. I secured it without bothering to hide it like on my previous mission.

"I'm really glad I'm up here with you, Macie," he said. "We'll be fine."

He checked the device again anyway.

Adrien smiled at me. I had only been back in Uptown for a few days, but I had nearly forgotten how comforting his eyes could be.

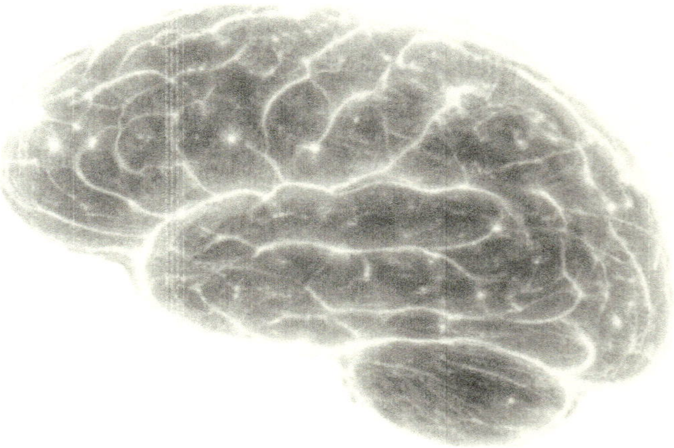

Chapter Twenty

Inside The Beast

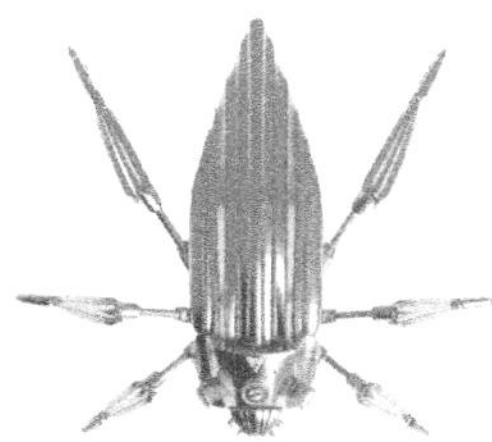

I had triggered something I couldn't see.

The elevator ground to a halt on the ninth level of the complex. Adrien and the team had decided that skipping the rest of Uptown was the safest way to avoid any executives who might take a second look when we walked by. The ninth level was supposed to be office space, according to one of the maps from the Nanotech database I had accessed, though we had not been able to confirm whether those maps were accurate. Not until now.

Adrien and I stepped out and attempted to appear nonchalant as we scanned the cubicles around us. The automatic lights had been off when we arrived, but quickly turned on with a wave of my arms. The offices and hallways nearest to the elevator were completely deserted, with files and food wrappers scattered across cubicle desks. Adrien set his bag down on one of the desks and began working at the datascreen in the corner.

The computers on this level would have had clearance as high as mine on Level Twelve, but we did not have to worry about regular security checks in these offices. I did not pretend to know exactly what Adrien was doing, but I had seen him work enough at headquarters to understand that whatever he was doing would get someone at Nanotech into serious trouble.

I guess headquarters really was home for me now. It was where I could rest most easily, surrounded by my family. What a strange thing to think about in the Nanotech complex, of all places.

Lights flashed across the datascreen as Adrien worked, pressing seemingly random buttons and jamming what looked like bent pencils into datastick ports. I decided to search through the physical files in one of the private offices rather than stand idle.

I cringed at the disorganization after opening several over-stuffed file drawers. The datapads and folders were shoved both vertically and horizontally, with folded corners and scratched screens. They were not even arranged alphabetically. They seemed to be loosely organized by size, though. I flipped through a drawer, pushing aside files that only contained fi-nancial reports from the last plastic bag shipment.

A datapad labeled *Nanobot Shipment–Quarter One* caught my attention. I tapped the edge of the screen and flipped through the first few pages. I could not immediately identify anything unusual, but I knew I could analyze it further back at head-quarters. I slipped the datapad into my briefcase.

"I've got it all set up. You ready to keep going?" Adrien called from the other room.

I stepped out of the office and nodded. "Yeah. Let's get going before the cleaning crews start."

Adrien gathered his equipment and moved toward the elevator. I followed close behind.

The next three levels mirrored the ninth. Storage and office spaces stretched endlessly, filled with rows of gray cubicles and dormant screens. I found myself unexpectedly grateful that, despite everything, my office had a window. These spaces would never appear in the glossy marketing pamphlets handed out during Nanotech orientation.

The fifth level was the first to break the pattern, though only slightly. It housed an advanced care unit, stocked with white crates of nanobot injections and IV fluid bags. This was where Uptown residents, and the wealthiest from Midtown, received treatment, though they likely entered through offices above. I doubted many of them knew how far down their care extended.

Adrien had little to do on the medical levels, so I focused on memorizing everything I could–serial numbers, nanobot counts, patient registrations. It was too dangerous to record anything externally. My memory was the only safe storage.

We moved downward quickly. With so many civilians passing through, it was unlikely we would uncover anything the rebellion did not already know. Adrien's work on Level Nine would be far more valuable than anything I could gather there.

After sweeping through Levels Four and Three, we reached the lowest accessible floor. At least, the lowest one the elevator would allow.

We entered Level Two quietly, careful to avoid the security cameras we could see, and guessing at the ones we could not.

Avoiding all of them was impossible, but we minimized exposure as best we could.

Level Two was filled with medical equipment and plastic-wrapped tables. I recognized the space immediately from the images I had been shown my first day at headquarters. This was where the experiments took place, and where bodies were kept out of sight.

Adrien looked around grinning. "This reminds me of Matthew's bunker. I never knew he had so much in common with Nanotech."

"He has a bunker?" I gasped.

"Sure, he hid it in the basement of his apartment building. It's actually just behind the Grub-Mart."

I leaned against one wall, taking in the space and committing every detail to memory, when the other elevator chimed.

Before I could react, Adrien was beside me.

We dove behind a med screen.

Chapter Twenty-One

Cornered

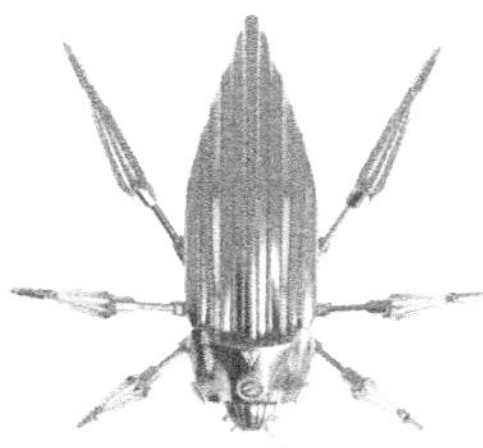

The change wasn't subtle anymore.

Huddling behind the med screen, I felt Adrien's warm breath against my cheek, short and jagged. I reached for his arm as the elevator doors slid open. He did not pull away.

Three figures stepped out. I didn't recognize the first two. They were both large and carried sonic weapons at the ready, theire safety lights turned off. The came Mr. Anderson. My breath caught as he moved into the light, his guards forming a loose triangle behind him. Adrien whispered something to me, but I didn't catch it.

Mr. Anderson's piercing eyes swept the room. He watched people the way others read reports–quickly, thoroughly, and without emotion. I could have sworn he looked directly at me, but he did nothing.

One of the guards turned to him, gesturing around the room with his weapon as if daring us to act first. Mr. Anderson responded with a small, sweeping motion of his hand. The search began. The guard on the left moved methodically through the room, checking between crates I assumed were filled with nanobots.

A sharp tug on my arm pulled my attention back. Adrien met my eyes, worry breaking through his usual calm. He leaned in again, and this time I heard him.

"Macie, we have to go. Now!" he hissed.

I shook my head, pulling him further behind the med screen. "No, we've come this far, and now we can get even more information," I replied.

Adrien pointed across the room. One of the guards was looking our way, sonic weapon raised. The size of the lab did nothing to ease the chill that ran through me when I saw the weapon angled in our direction.

I turned back to Adrien. "Maybe your plan is better," I admitted.

He did not react beyond tightening his grip on my hand as he scanned the room for an exit.

We spotted the elevator at the same time. I had never been so relieved to see a massive set of metal doors. Adrien risked a glance into the open space, checking for Mr. Anderson or the guards. We could not see them. It was our only chance.

Still holding my hand, Adrien ran. He pulled me up so suddenly that I stumbled before finding my footing. As I moved, the comm piece fell from my ear and bounced away. I didn't stop to look for it. I ran. I did not look back. Even if they had seen us, they could not know my face. My identity would ruin everything.

The elevator doors slid open automatically as we approached, the sensor flashing white. We dove inside. I hit the metal floor hard, the impact forcing a groan from my chest. Adrien slammed the "Level Eight" button before dropping beside me.

Pain spread across my ribs as I tested my breathing. Bruises were already forming beneath my clothes. Adrien steadied me, his hand firm against my back as he helped me sit up.

“Everything intact?” he asked, searching my face.

“I think so. Maybe that training with Emmalyn is actually doing something,” I said.

A laugh slipped out, and I immediately regretted it, clutching my side as pain flared. Adrien smirked, then flattened his expression when I shot him a look.

The elevator chimed softly as we reached our level. Adrien pulled out a small datascreen and began transferring everything we had gathered to the network back at headquarters.

I hesitated, then spoke.

“Hey, Adrien, do you think you can connect my comm piece to the main servers?”

“Yes, why?” he asked.

“I dropped it behind the med screen on Level Two. Maybe we could hear what Mr. Anderson is doing down there.”

Adrien lifted his head slowly and met my eyes.

“Macie.”

I braced myself for a reprimand.

“That is some great last-minute thinking!” he said, already typing furiously into his datapad.

I let out a breath I had not realized I was holding.

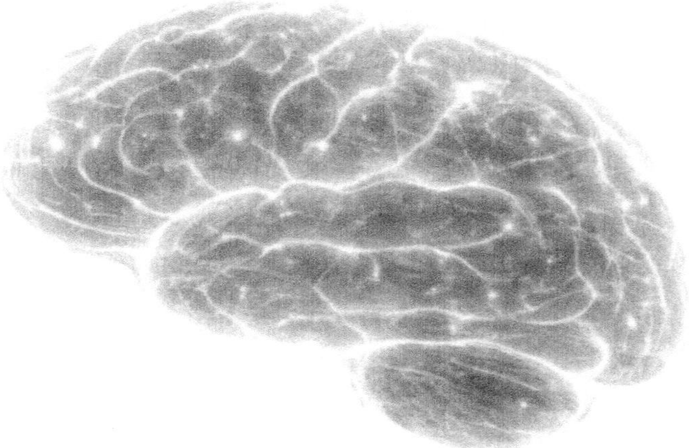

Chapter Twenty-Two

A Fragile Alliance

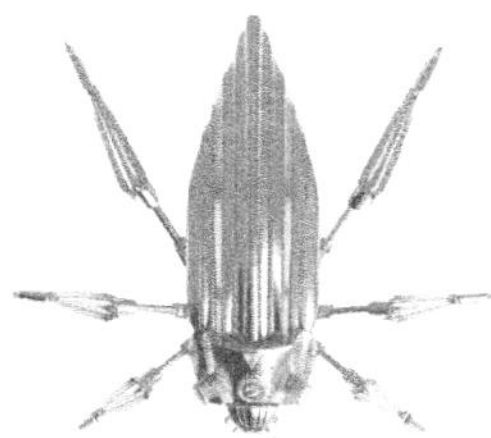

I had become the error.

Adrien and I exited the Nanotech complex on the eighth level, avoiding Uptown to reduce the risk of being recognized. Our business attire blended into Midtown far better than the black vest and multi-pocketed jacket I had worn before.

We returned to headquarters with all the data we had collected and went straight to the server room. Adrien connected his datapad to one of the computers and began transferring everything. Some of it was finally starting to connect. The more evidence we gathered, the easier it would be to show the public the truth. We sifted through images, files, and recordings, compiling them onto a single datapad. It struggled under the weight of the information, lagging as we scrolled.

We brought the compiled data to Dr. Bethel in her study, where she sat reviewing footage from Simon's Lin City Guard bodycam.

"What's this?" she asked, scrolling through the files.

"It's everything we were able to confirm at Nanotech today. Everything we can show people," Adrien said.

"We need to present this to the rest of the team, but first, Macie needs to return to Uptown. She's been gone too often," Dr. Bethel said.

Adrien nodded.

"Do I have to go now?" I asked. I would not admit it to the others, but I preferred sleeping at headquarters over my apartment in Uptown.

Dr. Bethel's expression told me the decision was final. She called for Emmalyn and handed her the datapad.

"Take a look at this. We're planning to send Macie back to Uptown with a wire. Do you have any thoughts?"

Emmalyn shook her head. "That's fine. But if I could send her with a weapon, I'd feel better."

Dr. Bethel agreed, and Emmalyn led me out of the office. I had carried weapons before, but I had never used one. No one had ever given me a reason to.

We stopped outside the armory and entered after Emmalyn unlocked the door. Only a few people knew the code, and I turned my head as she entered it. The room was lined with racks of weapons, many of them outdated compared to what Lin City guards carried. I was only authorized to use the smallest ones. Emmalyn and Simon had made that clear. I did not argue.

Emmalyn shut the door behind us and moved toward one of the racks, scanning the selection. I waited. I did not know enough to choose for myself. She handed me a compact weapon, small enough to fit in my pocket, and began explaining its use.

She was methodical, repeating each step until I could recite it back without hesitation. I understood the need for caution, but the repetition still felt excessive. I kept that to myself.

We stayed longer than necessary. Emmalyn moved from weapon to weapon, describing tools I might one day need. Some were sonic devices designed to incapacitate targets with directed sound. Others looked like relics from another era, including something that resembled a rocket launcher. I doubted Dr. Bethel would allow something like that in the armory, but I was no longer sure what limits existed here.

When Emmalyn was satisfied, we returned to the foyer. Adrien was waiting, holding an earpiece and a bundle of wires. I had worn one before, hidden beneath layers of tactical gear. This time, it would sit beneath my suit.

Emmalyn worked the wire carefully into my hair. She assured me it was secure, invisible. I nodded, but as I prepared to ascend through Lin City, I could not shake the feeling that it was still exposed.

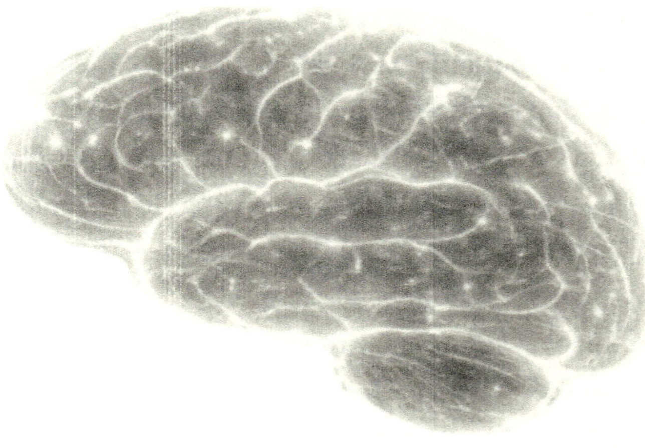

Chapter Twenty-Three

Clear Message

Lin City wasn't what it claimed to be.

I fiddled with my earpiece as I reached the Uptown entrance. My hair was long enough to cover it, but I still worried someone would notice the wire and report me. I handed my ID badge to the guard. He did not react to my earpiece, the power source in my pocket, or the weapon. The scanner blinked green.

The gate slid open, and I moved through quickly, slipping my badge back into my pocket. I glanced over my shoulder, half-expecting to be stopped, but the guards had already returned to scanning the catwalks. The speakers in Uptown emitted their usual artificial cricket sounds, and city cleaners scrubbed the streets with lemon-scented solution and white mops. That scent used to reassure me. Now it only reminded me how carefully Nanotech controlled everything, including me.

The hour should have meant empty streets, but there were still gatherings. I avoided any crowds where they appeared.

When I reached my apartment, I slipped inside without hesitation. Even the enclosed stairwell felt safer than the open streets. I took the stairs, passing my neighbors' doors. Laughter echoed faintly through the particle-wood walls, a reminder of who we were trying to protect.

I held my arm up to the scanner. The lock clicked, and the door slid open. My smile disappeared the moment I stepped inside.

I froze.

My apartment building had been destroyed. Furniture was torn apart, curtains ripped down, everything overturned. I dropped my bag and moved through the space, searching for anything intact. Clothes were scattered across the bedroom. Mirrors had been ripped from the walls and shattered across the floor. I barely noticed the glass under my feet as I assessed the damage.

I emptied my briefcase and began filling it with whatever remained usable: a jacket, my grandmother's earrings, silverware, a first aid kit. I moved quickly, forcing myself not to think.

Then I saw it.

A small glint of light on the ruined countertop.

A datastick.

I picked it up and turned it over in my hand. One side bore the Nanotech logo. The other held a message written in fine black ink. Mr. Anderson's handwriting.

Macie. I had high hopes for you. I do hope we watch a sunset together again.

The words were cramped, but unmistakable. I held the datastick above my datapad for a moment, my hand hovering. If I opened it, there was no going back.

I exhaled slowly and inserted the drive. The screen lit up, flooding my vision with brightness.

Files. Hundreds of them.

Each labeled with a date and a location, starting with the first time I had gone to headquarters alone.

My breath caught as I scrolled. Images of me walking toward headquarters. Images of me with Emmalyn. With Simon.

With Adrien.

We were laughing. Smiling. Unaware.

I had documented our own destruction.

I shoved the datapad and datastick into my bag and grabbed a shard of broken mirror. Ignoring the sting in my hand, I moved through the apartment, finding every camera. I cut wires, smashed lenses, destroyed everything that could still be watching me.

Before breaking the last camera, I stopped.

Then I turned the glass on myself.

I clenched my teeth as I drove the shard into the flesh beneath my elbow. The sound of it breaking skin was soft, almost wet, and my pulse roared in my ears as I forced myself deeper. Pain surged, sharp and immediate, but I did not stop. I dug until I felt it.

The chip.

There was no reason to keep it anymore. I was not going back.

Blood ran down my arm as I pulled it free. I had always thought I was afraid of blood. I wasn't. Not anymore.

I bandaged the wound as best I could, my hands steady despite everything.

When I finished, I pulled on the jacket I had salvaged and drew the hood tight around my face. Surveillance cameras and drones filled the path between my apartment and headquarters. I would not make it easy for them.

Dr. Bethel would know what to do. I was sure of it.

Chapter Twenty-Four

COMPROMISED

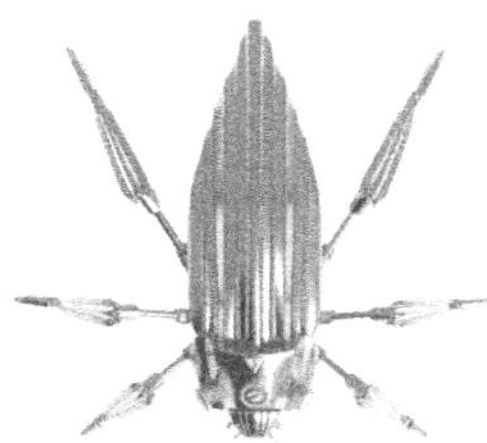

The system wasn't failing—it was succeeding.

By the time I made it back to headquarters on Level Five, I was barely able to breathe. I had sprinted most of the levels, adrenaline pushing me down the stairs. When I arrived, a line of Downtown residents stretched out the door, blocking the regular morning flow. The soup kitchen was clearly working. It was bringing people together, just as Stephen had said it would.

Stephen stood at the entrance, greeting each person with a smile. He made an effort to remember faces, to treat each per-son like they mattered. His smile faded when he saw me. I was supposed to be in Uptown. My presence here was a problem.

I gestured for him to step aside with me.

People in line watched as we moved to a quieter corner. I could feel their eyes on me. My heeled shoes, my pressed jack-et–I did not belong here. I wondered if any of them recognized me from the broadcasts, standing beside the man who helped keep them controlled. The thought made my stomach turn.

Stephen spoke first, his voice low and urgent.

"What are you doing here? Do Emmalyn and Bethel know?"

I shook my head, trying to steady my breathing.

"No one knows yet. My apartment–and the location of headquarters–has been compromised," I said.

Stephen's expression shifted, sharpening.

"What do you need?"

I pulled the datastick from my bag. "I need Adrien. And I need this saved before it wipes."

Stephen glanced toward the entrance, where the line was growing restless. He nodded.

"Go."

I did not hesitate. I pushed through the doors, brushing past people without apology.

Adrien was in the dining hall, sanitizing pots of water on the stove. Simon was nearby. After the water cooled, he transferred it into plastic bottles for distribution.

Simon noticed me first. He tapped Adrien's shoulder.

They both stared.

Adrien crossed the room quickly and grabbed my shoulder.

"Macie, what's wrong?"

"We have to get this onto your system," I said.

I pressed the datastick into his hand and closed his fingers around it. He understood immediately.

We left together. I did not let go of his hand.

Adrien shut the door to his room behind us and powered on the monitors. White light flooded the space. He opened his hand, revealing the datastick and the faint mark it had left in his skin.

"Where did you get this?" he asked.

"It was left in my apartment. I don't think it was an accident. Someone wanted me to find it. Someone wanted all of us to see it."

Adrien hesitated, then inserted the drive.

A prompt appeared. He accepted it.

The screens filled instantly.

Images. Videos. Messages. Screenshots.

All of me.

I saw myself from angles I had never seen before. Walking. Talking. Smiling. My hair, my posture, my expressions–all captured in perfect detail.

In one frame, I was smiling at something off-camera, unaware of the lens watching me.

I sank to the floor.

My hands covered my face as I struggled to breathe. The room spun.

Adrien knelt in front of me and gently pulled my hands away. He did not speak right away. He did not need to.

Everything had changed.

"These are surveillance logs," he said finally, glancing at the screens. "We always knew something like this could happen. It's not your fault."

I wiped at my face, trying to steady myself.

"How can I stay if I can't go back?" I asked.

I had no role here anymore. The safest thing I could do for them was leave.

Adrien shook his head.

"No one's going to make you leave. Bea and Simon wouldn't allow it. Not even Emmalyn would risk losing you."

I almost smiled at that. Adrien let out a quiet laugh.

"We should get Dr. Bethel," he said. "I want to make sure you're safe."

I nodded.

Maybe they would understand. Maybe I could still help.

Emmalyn joined us in the server room, and we went through everything again. She kept her expression controlled, but I could see the tension beneath it.

Emmalyn's eyes lingered on one of the images a fraction too long before she looked away.

"Emmalyn, can you get Dr. Bethel?" I asked.

I needed her there. I needed direction.

"Dr. Bethel became ill shortly after you left. It's better if she rests," Emmalyn said, as she shook her head.

Adrien had not told me. I glanced at him. Dr. Bethel had been fine when I left. A tightness settled in my chest that had nothing to do with running.

"What happened?" I asked. "Could it be her nanobot implants? If Nanotech knows about me, they might know about her too."

Emmalyn shook her head, then paused, considering.

"Bea is with her now. We need to focus on this," she said, gesturing to the screens.

I nodded, though my thoughts were already spiraling.

Emmalyn fired questions at me–who left the datastick, who could have exposed me, when Nanotech might have found out.

I had no answers.

None of it made sense.

Why had Mr. Anderson kept me in place if he knew?

Maybe he had not known at first.

Maybe he knew everything.

I did not know which possibility was worse.

My thoughts blurred together as Adrien and Emmalyn continued talking. Their voices faded into noise.

All I could think about was him.

And what he would do when he finally decided I was no longer useful.

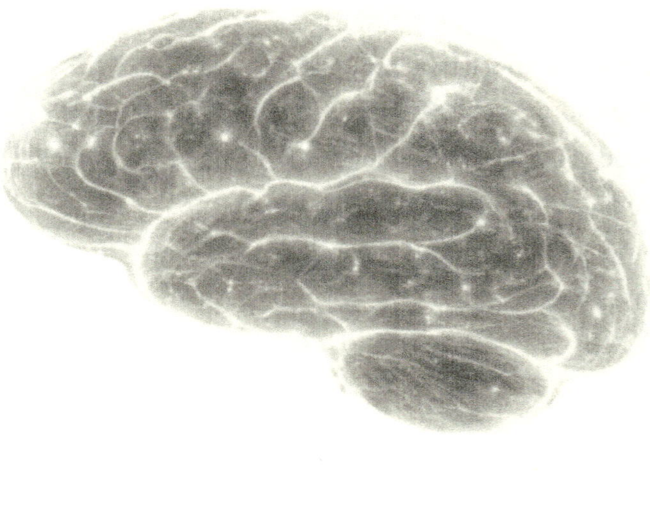

Chapter Twenty-Five

A New Day

I made a choice they couldn't reverse.

I waited until I could not hear any movement beyond my bedroom door before going to find Dr. Bethel. Her room was bathed in warm light and smelled of herby stew. She sat propped up against a pile of pillows and looked at me as I entered. I was relieved to see her awake.

"Macie, what are you doing here?" Dr. Bethel asked. Her voice was hoarse, but still gentle.

"I'm worried about you. We all are," I said, kneeling beside the bed.

Dr. Bethel shook her head. "I am old, and I have lived a life of stress. I hope you will never have to endure the same."

I did not know how to respond. I had come looking for answers about her illness. Instead, I found resignation. She had always been warm, steady. Now she looked diminished, distant in a way I had never seen before.

A scream tore through the building.

Dr. Bethel tried to sit up, but I pressed her back against the pillows. I hurried out, pulling the door shut behind me.

Emmalyn and Simon were already in the foyer, crouched on either side of a sobbing woman. I slowed, trying to understand what was happening, but neither of them acknowledged me.

A moment later, Stephen and Adrien rushed in, both out of breath.

"It's Matthew's sister," Stephen said, moving toward her. "What happened, Carrie?"

"He's gone, Stephen," she cried. "They found him."

"What do you mean gone? Where is Matthew?"

Carrie shoved a datapad toward him. Stephen's face drained of color as he looked at the screen. I stepped closer, catching a glimpse over his shoulder.

Matthew lay motionless. Blood pooled beneath him. His skin was split in thin, jagged lines, as if something had torn him apart from the inside.

"His nanobots," Adrien said quietly, turning away.

Stephen left with Carrie, the datapad slipping from his hands onto the floor.

Silence settled over the room.

Then Emmalyn spoke.

"We need to attack now. This is an act of aggression that can't be ignored."

There was something sharp in her voice, not just anger, but something almost eager. I stared at her. We did not have the numbers. We were barely holding together as it was.

Simon shook his head. "How can you say that? We aren't ready. Dr. Bethel said–"

"I don't care what she said!" Emmalyn snapped. "I'm your leader now. We can't lose someone and keep hiding. They know who we are. They know where we are. It's only a matter of time before they come for all of us."

Simon fell silent. I did not know what to say, or if I should say anything at all.

Emmalyn stormed out, leaving the rest of us behind.

Adrien glanced at Simon. "She's just angry, right? We could leave? Scatter to different provinces?"

Simon stood abruptly. "Or maybe she's right. We've been waiting long enough. I'm ready to do something."

The mood in the dining hall felt heavier than it had before. Emmalyn spoke with Stephen in one corner while Carrie sat alone at a table. I moved to sit beside her.

"Matthew was a great man. I'm so sorry," I said.

Carrie looked at me, her eyes red and unfocused.

"He wanted to tell everyone about this so badly," she said. "I just wanted him to hide. To protect himself."

She gave a weak smile. "He used to talk about building a bunker in his apartment. Said he could disappear if I ever convinced him."

Her voice broke. "I wish he had listened."

I nodded, but the words I wanted would not come. If I had never stayed, if I had never been found, maybe he would still be alive.

Across the room, Emmalyn and Stephen's quiet conversation rose into something sharper. Adrien and Simon stepped in. I did not hear what Simon said, but it ended the exchange.

Emmalyn turned to the group, her voice carrying across the room.

"We have to retaliate against Nanotech. We have to try. They will keep taking from us until we stop them."

I looked around at the faces in the room. Fear. Anger. Grief. But on top of all of that? Resolve.

Chapter Twenty-Six

THE LAST STAND

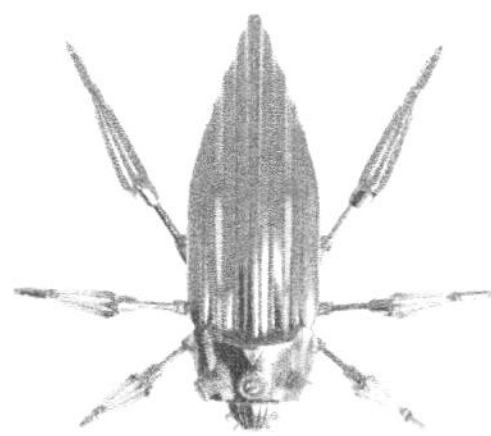

They weren't prepared for this version of me.

Emmalyn insisted we begin preparations immediately. She sent Simon to collect weapons from the rebellion's makeshift armory Downtown and left Adrien and me to cross-reference the water reserves with known entrances into Nanotech's lower buildings. If we could move through the empty reserves, we might stay undetected. Bea joined us a few hours later, ready to assist Simon and Stephen with the weapons.

I would be going into the water system with the others. Adrien would stay behind. I tried not to dwell on the fact that he would be almost alone at headquarters, aside from Dr. Bethel, who was still confined to bed. It was difficult to talk about anything other than Emmalyn's plan, but I knew he did not believe in it. Whenever we were alone, he reminded me how dangerous it was, how unprepared we were.

"We could leave now," he said, sitting on the floor of my room, sorting through datapads. "Catch a train to one of the outer cities."

"You know we have to do this," I said, looking up from the map in my hands. "I wish it were that simple. But this is for Lin City, Adrien."

I did not want to say it. I did not want to believe it. But I said it anyway.

Adrien did not respond.

We left headquarters just after sunset, avoiding the busiest parts of Downtown. The streets were nearly empty, and those we did pass turned away quickly. Darkness worked in our favor when we reached the Level Four entrance to the water reserves. No one would see us enter. No one would question the wall once it sealed behind us.

I entered the memorized code into the control panel and exhaled when the entrance opened. I had feared the codes might have changed, but I had not voiced that doubt with Emmalyn beside me.

She led us inside, following the route Adrien and I had mapped. We moved in single file, Bea at the rear. The tunnels were nearly silent.

Water dripped from the ceiling, remnants of a system that had once sustained the entire city.

We had not been walking long when Emmalyn raised her hand. We stopped immediately. I was about to ask why when I heard it.

A low, building roar.

White noise swelled in my ears. Every muscle in my body locked as the sound rushed toward us. Bea's expression shifted first.

"They've opened the dams," she said. "It's water."

The surge hit moments later.

Water tore around the corner and slammed into us with crushing force. I collided with Bea, the impact knocking the breath from my lungs. The current dragged me away from the ledge, my body spinning as I fought for control.

I forced my arms forward, pushing against the current. Pain shot through my shoulder, but I did not stop. Training took over. Fear and instinct blurred together as I fought to stay above the surface.

Then something caught my arm.

I was pulled free of the current and dragged onto a ledge. I scrambled forward, gasping, and turned. Stephen released his grip on me.

We collapsed onto the concrete, soaked and shaking.

Bea was gone.

I pushed myself to my feet and reached for the control panel beside the door. Before I could touch it, the entrance slid open.

Mr. Anderson stood waiting.

Behind him, a line of Lin City guards raised their weapons in perfect formation.

The others rose beside me, just as stunned. No one spoke.

Then Mr. Anderson did.

"Thank you, Emmalyn. Why don't you all come in?"

I turned to her, waiting for denial, for anything.

She said nothing.

Emmalyn stepped forward and joined the guards.

I moved after her without thinking, anger cutting through the shock, but Stephen caught my arm and pulled me back.

Before I could react, he shoved me.

I fell into the rushing water, instinct barely giving me time to take a breath before it swallowed me.

Chapter Twenty-Seven

Washed Away

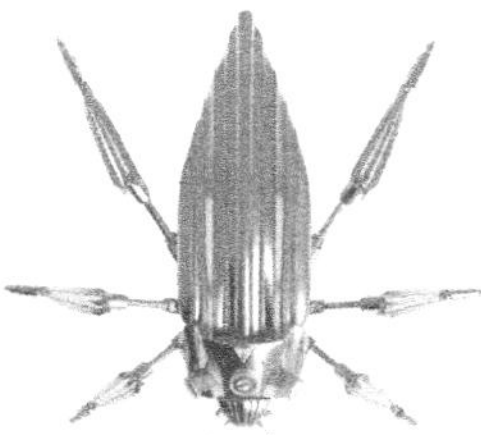

The system moved to erase me.

The water dragged me back toward the entrance, and the sound of weapon fire faded behind me. For a moment, I wondered if I should stop fighting. Let the current take me. Whatever waited beyond these tunnels would be worse than anything I could imagine.

But I did not stop.

My arms thrashed as I fought for control in the churning water. Pain shot through my shoulder, but I clenched my teeth and pushed forward. Stephen trusted me to do this. I had to believe that meant something.

The current slammed me into the walls, knocking the breath from my lungs. Water filled my mouth. I did not want to think about what I was swallowing.

The tunnels were nearly pitch black. I could not tell if my head was above the surface or below it. Sound blurred into a constant roar.

I reached blindly for the wall, groping for anything I could grab. A ledge meant a door. A door meant escape.

My knuckles scraped against rough concrete. I ignored the pain. I could not think about who I had left behind.

Then my hand struck something solid.

A ledge.

I grabbed it, and every muscle in my body strained as I pulled myself upward. My head broke the surface, and I gasped for air, clinging to the edge.

There was a door.

A control panel sat beside it, glowing faintly.

I reached for it, my grip slipping against the wet surface. I entered one code.

Error.

Another.

Error.

Again.

Error.

Tears blurred my vision as I kept trying. The edge cut into my palms, and I felt blood mix with the rushing water below.

I slammed my hand against the panel.

Maybe I screamed. I could not hear it over the water.

Then–

The panel flashed.

The door opened.

Light cut into the darkness, a thin, blinding line.

I forced myself forward, dragging my body through the opening. My limbs trembled as I collapsed into the alley beyond. I coughed violently, water spilling from my lungs as I fought to breathe.

A small group of Nanotech workers stared at me from a distance. No one moved.

I pushed myself against the wall and forced my legs to hold me. One of them stepped closer, reaching out.

I shoved her away.

"Don't," I rasped.

There were cameras everywhere. I could not risk it.

After a moment, I steadied myself enough to move. The streets were nearly empty. I stumbled around for what felt like hours. When I finally got my bearings, I returned to Level Five. Grub Mart's lights flickered in the distance, and the blue streetlights cast everything in a sterile glow.

Then I saw it.

A crowd had gathered ahead.

I forced my way through, leaving streaks of blood on uniforms as I passed. When I reached the front, I stopped.

Headquarters was gone.

Burned out. Hollow.

Ash coated the ground where walls had once stood.

My mind struggled to process what I was seeing. Where was the server room?

Where was Adrien?

I turned, searching the crowd for anyone I recognized. Faces stared back, concerned but unfamiliar. No one knew what this place had been. No one understood what had been lost.

I stumbled into the wreckage.

Again, I searched for anything that remained.

Cans. A datapad. Fragments of what used to be something more.

I gathered what I could carry and forced myself to leave. Surviving the tunnels had been luck. I would not test it again.

I stopped just beyond the ruins.

Where could I go?

Guards would be everywhere. Even without knowing my face, they would stop someone who looked like me–soaked, bleeding, unstable.

I turned down a catwalk.

And then I knew.

Matthew's bunker was cramped and dark, but it gave me a view of the city. One wall was covered in screens, each connected to a different security feed. Some were dark, disconnected, but most still flickered with life.

I did not know how long I could stay there.

But I needed time.

Time to heal.

Time to think.

Time to decide what came next.

I told myself I was safe.

But somewhere deep inside, I knew better.

They could still find me.

And if they did, this would be the end of everything.

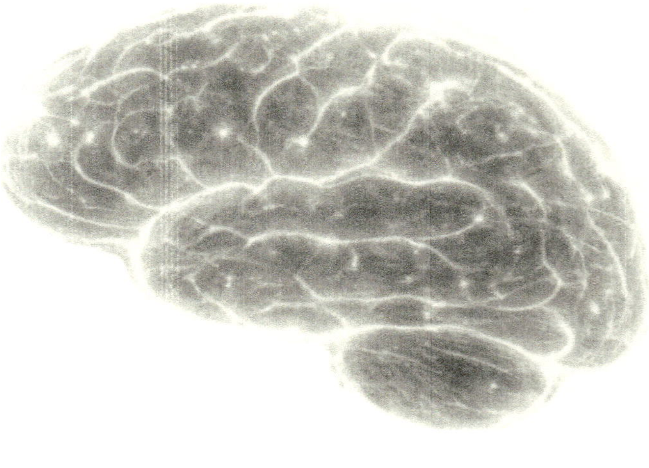

Chapter Twenty-Eight

Remnants

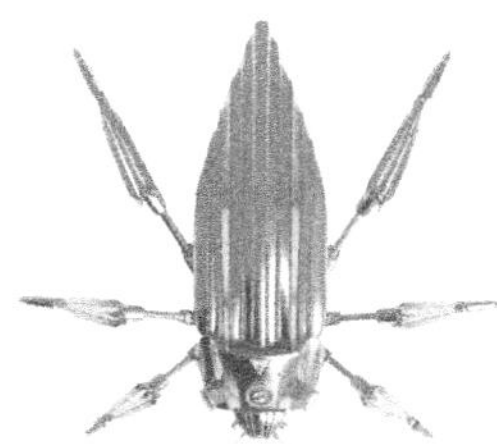

Everything came apart at once.

The walls of my self-made prison seemed to close tighter around me the longer I stayed. Not speaking to anyone had left my voice hoarse and my throat dry. Sometimes I whispered to myself just to make sure I still could. When I was not doing that, I slept in short bursts and only ate when it was necessary. I had no idea how long I had been there. I tracked the first few days by watching the shift between day and night through the remaining security feeds, but eventually, everything blurred together. An endless cycle of dehydration and observation. Watching the city that used to be my home.

Every time I thought about where I was, I felt Matthew's presence behind me. He had known something would happen. He had prepared. This bunker was the last remnant of the rebellion. No one else knew it existed. The rebellion had been nothing more than whispers in a city of noise. I had no way of tracking those I had left behind in the tunnels. No way of knowing if any of them were still alive. I was surrounded by data and had nothing I could do with it. I had learned how to navigate parts of the system, but I could not access anything inside Nanotech. Not without Adrien.

I spent hours searching through the stored files, reviewing old member profiles, trying to understand why Emmalyn had done what she did. To me. To all of us. I wanted to understand why Ellis Anderson wanted to live forever, and why he was willing to destroy everyone else to do it. I wanted to understand why Dr. Bethel, Adrien, Stephen, and the others had trusted me when they knew I could lead to their destruction.

And I wanted to understand why I was still alive.

Why me?

What had I done to deserve it when they had not?

The questions never stopped.

I barely slept. I rationed my food. I waited.

I did not know what I was waiting for, but I knew I had not survived this long just to give up.

A screen flickered.

Another camera feed went dark.

I leaned forward, cursing under my breath. I had not even seen what caused it. Nanotech could have shut it down, or it could have failed on its own. I had no way of knowing.

The thought settled in immediately.

If Anderson could trace the feeds, he could find me.

And if he found me, I was dead.

Everything we had built would disappear with me.

I shifted back against the wall, trying to steady my breathing.

Even staying hidden was no longer sustainable. My water had run out days ago. The only moisture I had left came from the liquid in the canned food I rationed.

I almost laughed.

Matthew had planned for everything except that.

Another flicker.

A motion alert.

I turned toward the screen.

The camera feed showed the corridor just outside the bunker.

Someone was there.

Emmalyn.

She knocked on the door.

I froze.

How did she find me?

I stayed silent.

She knocked again.

"Macie, I know you're in there," she said. "I need your help. Please open the door."

I did not move.

She would not take me like she had taken the others.

But I could not stay here much longer.

Emmalyn sank to her knees.

"Please, Macie. I want to fix this. I want us to work together again."

I said nothing.

Then—

"Adrien is alive."

I opened the door.

Emmalyn looked up at me from the floor. Her face was streaked with tears.

"You smell like shit," she said.

"I know," I replied, stepping aside to let her in. "Where is he?"

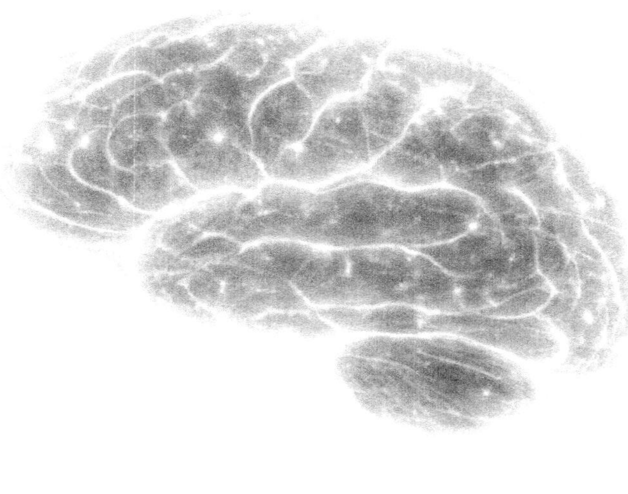

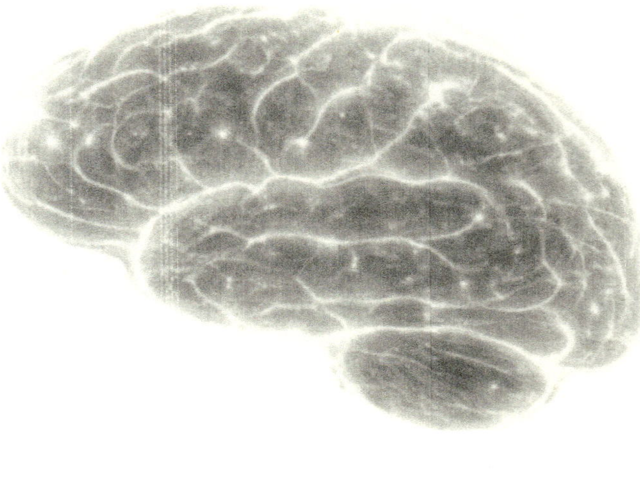

About Ivy Ru

IVY RU is a high school and college student living in Minnesota, graduating just as this first novel in your hands is released . . . and she is also your new favorite author!

Ivy has been writing for as long as she can remember, her first short stories being about her imaginary little sister, Sinnamon.

Now, Ivy has moved on from realistic fiction to suspense and sci-fi. Ivy loves that she can say writing is her job and hopes that she will be able to for many years to come.

When Ivy's not writing, she enjoys playing the harp, drums, and piano, as well as practicing multiple dance styles, and she's excited to dip her toes into politics in college.

If you want to get updates on all of Ivy's publications and adventures, please subscribe to her newsletter:

www.IvyRuWrites.com/witb

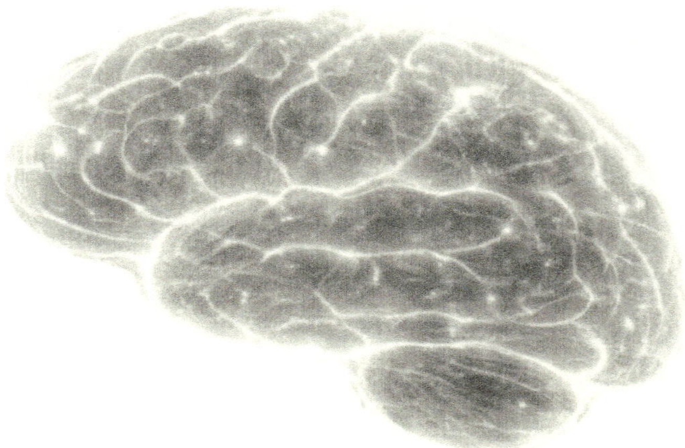

Acknowledgements

I would like to acknowledge all of my mentors who have helped me start my writing career, whether they are other authors, editors, friends, or family. Thank you Jeri Shepherd, Tiffany Rose Nickel, Christopher Schmitz, Anthony Wedgeworth, and of course Mom and Dad. I would not have been able to write this novel without the help I received from all of you.

Ivy's Mom, Ivy, and Jeri Shepherd - Publishing Contract Signed at the Twin Cities Con 2024

I want to give a special thanks to Jeri Shepherd, who has acted not only as my mentor, but also as my editor and publisher. You have helped me more than I could ever thank you with realizing my visions and getting them onto paper, or at least onto the computer screen!

Love Whispers In The Blue?

Check out these other IVY RU titles!

Made in the USA
Coppell, TX
04 May 2026

76625310R00100